A WOMAN
NAMED DAMARIS

JANETTE OKE

A WOMAN
NAMED DAMARIS

JO

A WOMAN NAMED DAMARIS
A Literary Express, Inc. Book
(a subsidiary of Doubleday Direct, Inc.)
Reprinted by special arrangement with:
Bethany House Publishers
A Ministry of Bethany Fellowship International

PRINTING HISTORY
A Bethany House Publication / August 1991
The Janette Oke Collection / 1997

If you would be interested in purchasing additional copies of this
book, or have any questions concerning the Janette Oke
Collection and your membership, or if you would like to
correspond with the author, please contact us at:

The Janette Oke Collection
Literary Express, Inc.
1540 Broadway
New York, NY 10036
Telephone #973-473-4800

ISBN: 1-58165-136-8

Printed in the United States of America

To Josue and Judith,
my Compassion kids.
May God bless your lives and help you
to be all He wants you to be.

———————

I began supporting Josue when he was quite young. He is now sixteen and a fine-looking young man. He lives in Mexico with his family and enjoys sports—especially soccer. He writes me short notes and draws me pictures. It has been interesting to share his growing up.

I met Judith when I traveled with Compassion to Haiti in January 1989. We visited some of the schools where Compassion children were scattered among the students.

The Haitian children were so open and loving, running to us to say hello, shake our hand, or to get a hug. I wondered how they could smile when they showed how hungry they were, lifting their simple shirts and showing us gaunt tummies. It was so sad. In that extremely needy country it was wonderful to see Compassion-sponsored children receiving schooling, health care, a daily meal, and most of all, the opportunity to hear about our Lord Jesus.

But there are not enough funds to meet all the needs. Many children are still without sponsorship.

Judith was one of the needy children. She lived with her

widowed grandmother, her mother having gone to Port au Prince in hope of finding some kind of work. Compassion decided to take on the care of Judith, and I was given the opportunity to provide her support.

Judith was shy—but sweet. We could not communicate with words, but I will never forget the little arm that wrapped around me. I fell in love with her then and hope that one day I will have the privilege of visiting her again.

Helping children through Compassion is a wonderful opportunity to share love. It amazes me that the organization is able to do so much with so little. Having seen the many other children in Haiti who have no such support, no proper meal to fill hungry tummies, no medical care when they are ill, no education to help them through life, no chance to hear the Gospel that will free them from the terrible fear of voodoo worship, I thank God that there are Compassion people who really care and give their lives to reaching out.

I am also thankful to be a small part of such a rewarding program. A few dollars makes it possible to turn a life around. I also have the privilege of remembering my children in prayer and communicating through letters. Compassion sends pictures and keeps me well informed of their welfare and growth.

God bless your work, Compassion!

Should you have an interest in being a part of the wonderful family of Compassion, you may write to them for information at one of the following addresses:

Compassion International   Compassion of Canada
3955 Cragwood Dr., Dept. A   Box 5591
PO Box 7000   London, Ontario
Colorado Springs, CO   N6A 9Z9
80933–0001

I'm sure you won't be disappointed.

JANETTE OKE was born in Champion, Alberta, during the depression years, to a Canadian prairie farmer and his wife. She is a graduate of Mountain View Bible College in Didsbury, Alberta, where she met her husband, Edward. They were married in May of 1957, and went on to pastor churches in Indiana as well as Calgary and Edmonton, Canada.

The Okes have three sons and one daughter and are enjoying the addition to the family of grandchildren. Edward and Janette have both been active in their local church, serving in various capacities as Sunday school teachers and board members. They make their home in Didsbury, Alberta.

Contents

Chapter One

Damaris

"Damaris! Damaris!"

Damaris Withers shrank back against the hard boards of the attic wall that supported her back. Pa was home, and she knew by his voice that he had been drinking. She wondered where he had found the money. She wished there was no such thing as money. It brought nothing but woe to the household.

"Damaris!" the man hollered again. "Where is thet girl?" he demanded, a nasty string of profanity following his second outburst.

Damaris shivered. She knew her pa would never find her in her attic retreat, but she never considered staying there. If she didn't go when called, things would not go well for her mother. Her pa would become angry and abusive. If she hurried, he might do no more than lash out with words, but if he became angry . . . The thought made Damaris shiver again.

She laid aside her book, worn from reading, and crawled from her hiding place. Silently she lowered herself to the beat-up chest that stood against the wall in her room and quietly replaced the trapdoor leading up to her hiding place. Then she stepped carefully onto the sagging cot that was her bed and down to the rag rug that covered the broken floorboard beside it. She slipped her feet into worn shoes, brushed at her mended dress to get rid of any cobwebs, and hastened toward the creaking stairs.

"Here I am," she said, trying hard to keep her voice from trembling.

Her father had settled himself in a chair by the table. One glance told Damaris that he had spent a good deal of his afternoon at the saloon. Fear gripped at her, but then a thought flashed through her mind. *If he's had plenty to drink, then maybe—maybe he will soon take to bed and leave Mama and me alone.*

"Get in here, girl!" roared her father. "Give yer poor ma a hand. Don't ya care a'tall thet she's got all the work to do?"

The man shook his head and began to curse again. "No respect a'tall," he ended his tirade.

"Yes, Pa," Damaris whispered.

No point telling him that already she had drawn water from the deep well for the two cows. That she had hoed the garden in the hot morning sun. That she had walked into town with the eggs and traded them for salt and flour. That she had chopped the wood for the fire and hauled the water to replenish the kitchen buckets. Or that Mama herself had given her permission to rest a few moments. All Damaris said was "Yes, Pa," as she moved forward to appease her irate father. To answer back or fail to show proper respect would get her the back of his hand at best or a thrashing if he felt so inclined.

He sat at the table mumbling his complaints and curses as Damaris and her mother scurried about the kitchen preparing him a hot meal. They did not dare speak. They did not even raise their eyes to each other. Nor did they look at the man slumped at the table. Damaris did not need to look. She had played this scene before—many times—whenever there was money from somewhere. She hated money. Hated what it did to her pa. Hated what it did to her mama. And she hated the fear coursing through her now, shriveling her body into a quaking, trembling mass.

"What's takin' ya so long?" her pa demanded, his words slurred and angry. "When a man gets home his supper oughta be waitin' fer 'im."

More angry words followed but Damaris tuned them out. She held the chipped plate for her mother to fill with pancakes and fried salted pork and hastened to the table to place it before her father.

"Where's the coffee?" he bellowed. Damaris returned quickly to the stove, hoping there had been time for the coffee to boil. There hadn't.

Her pa hated coffee that wasn't steaming. He also hated to wait. Which offense would be the most annoying on this night? Damaris glanced at her pa, hoping to be able to guess. One hand held the fork that shoveled the food to his mouth, the other shifted restlessly on the table. Damaris decided to risk the coffee—now. Perhaps he wouldn't notice that it was less than boiling. She poured a cup and hastened back to the table, then went for the sugar bowl. She held her breath as she entered the small cubicle that served as a pantry. Would he be angry? She glanced over her shoulder to see which objects from the table she might have to dodge if her father's anger turned violent.

He hadn't waited for the sugar. Lifting the cup to his lips, he took a drink. Immediately he turned, leaned from his chair, and spat the coffee onto the floor beside him.

"Tastes like slop," he said, accusing eyes glaring at Damaris. He turned his cup upside down and emptied the remainder of its contents onto the floor. But he did not throw the cup. For that Damaris was thankful.

"Bring me another one—hot—an' put some sugar in it!" he roared.

Damaris moved quickly to comply. The coffee was now boiling. Perhaps she had been lucky. The bit of stall had resulted in hot coffee, and her pa had remained reasonably controlled.

But her pa never drank the coffee. The hand that held the fork was slowly losing its grip, and a glaze started to cover the man's eyes. Damaris dared to glance at her mama. The man at the table would soon pass out, and it would be up to the two of them to get his dead weight from the kitchen floor to his bed. They had struggled with the weight of the big man many times. Damaris hated this part of the ordeal.

Slowly, the man slumped over the table. Damaris didn't know whether to step forward and risk holding him in his chair before he was totally unconscious, or to stand by and let him slide completely to the floor. It was always so much harder to lift him up after he had fallen. She raised her eyes to her mama and the woman nodded feebly. Damaris stepped forward and placed a hand on each of the man's shoulders, holding him against the back of his seat.

"I'll take his arms," she said softly to her mama in a remarkably controlled voice.

The slight woman moved forward, tugged off the man's heavy boots, tossed them aside, and lifted his legs.

Together they heaved and hoisted until they got him into the bedroom and finally managed to slide him onto his bed. Then they tossed the covers over the bulky frame.

Without a word they left the room and returned to the kitchen. Damaris pulled a rag from the scrub bucket and fell to her knees to wipe up the floor while her mama cleared the table.

Damaris glanced at the woman. Beads of perspiration still stood on her forehead, a reminder of the hard task of bedding her pa. She looked old for her thirty-four years. Old and tired. Yet Damaris knew from a picture tucked inside the little box in her mama's drawer that she had been young and attractive not many years before. Damaris thought she heard a deep sigh as the older woman placed the dirty plate in the dishpan on the stove.

"It's a shame to waste good coffee," her mama said quietly. "Want a cup?"

The coffee—when they had it—was kept for her pa or for the family's occasional guest. Damaris had tasted coffee only once before in her life. To be offered a cup now surprised her, but she nodded in assent, feeling a strange sensation of excitement. There slept her father, while she and her mama drank his coffee. Damaris stifled her impulse to giggle and went to wash her hands.

"Too bad we don't have some cake—or something," her mama said.

Damaris nodded again, the light leaping to her eyes.

She sipped her coffee, wondering why people made such a fuss about the bitter-tasting beverage. But Damaris would never have voiced such a negative opinion at that moment. She was set to savor every drop of the forbidden liquid.

"I like it much better with cream," her mama admitted. "Been so long since I had a cup—I'd most forgotten how it tastes."

Damaris took another sip. It was beginning to taste better. Perhaps because it was such a pleasure for the two of them to be sitting serenely at the table, completely composed and relaxed, knowing that it would be hours before her pa could be of any threat to them again.

"Were you reading?" her mama asked.

Damaris nodded, seeing in her mama's eyes complete understanding. She wondered how her mama knew, how they could communicate so completely with so few words.

"Wish we had some new books for you. You must have those few 'most worn out."

Damaris nodded again, but then hurried to add, "I don't mind. I always enjoy reading them again."

But deep in her heart, Damaris knew she would give almost anything to have some new books.

They sipped in silence for a few more minutes, then Mrs. Withers spoke again.

"You have pretty eyes," she said.

Damaris was not used to compliments—not even from her mama. She didn't know how to respond.

Her mama went on, "They are just like my papa's. He had dark brown eyes, too, you know. I took after Mama. My eyes are gray. I was always disappointed about that. Wanted dark eyes like my pa."

Damaris let her mama's words slide slowly past her. She had never given much thought to eyes. She supposed that gray ones could look out upon the world just as good as brown ones.

"One hasn't much choice about eyes, I guess," the woman mused aloud. "Shouldn't even waste time thinkin' 'bout it."

She stirred her coffee, her thoughts seeming to go on; then she took a deep breath and said, "One should be more concerned with things thet can be changed. Who we are—what we become—and how our lives affect others."

Damaris looked directly at her mama. The thin, pale woman sitting opposite her had slightly graying hair that was pushed haphazardly in a bun at the base of her neck. It had become dislodged in the struggle with her pa and several strands of shorter hair curled in wisps against her shallow cheeks. The longer strands had been tucked recklessly behind her ears. For the first time in her young life, Damaris wondered who her mama really was, and who she had been before she met and married her pa. Would life have been different if she had married someone else? Never married at all?

Damaris had never thought to ask such questions. She had accepted their life together as the way things were. Now she found herself wondering if there were alternatives. Could life have been different? For Mama? Even for her?

Her mama stirred in her chair. Damaris again lifted her eyes to look at her. For one brief moment the brown eyes met the gray and Damaris fancied that she saw something she had never seen before. She wasn't sure what it was or what it meant so she let her glance slip away.

"I have something I want you to have," the woman said. She rose quickly from the chair and left the room. She was gone for some time, and Damaris began wondering where she'd had to go to retrieve whatever it was she was after.

When she returned, her hair was even more dishevelled and bore bits of barn straw.

"I had it hid in the barn," she whispered. Damaris felt her eyes go toward the room where the man breathed heavily in his sleep.

Mrs. Withers produced a small piece of faded cloth tied tightly into a bundle. Damaris watched, her curiosity growing as her mama fumbled with the knots.

"Bring me my sewin' shears," the woman instructed, and Damaris crossed to the corner where the small basket of mending supplies was kept and returned almost on tiptoe.

The small packet held two articles. One was a pocket watch. Mrs. Withers lifted it tenderly, caressing it with her eyes before she extended it to Damaris.

"Your grandfather's," she said softly. "He gave it to me the night before he died."

There were tears in her eyes. Damaris couldn't fully understand the reason.

"Here," her mama prompted. "Take it."

Damaris hesitated, realizing in her limited way just how much the keepsake meant to her mama. Damaris hadn't known that her mama had anything totally her own. Even her few books had been unselfishly passed on to her daughter.

"Take it," her mama repeated, thrusting the watch toward Damaris again.

"But—"

"I want you to have it—and this too," said Mrs. Withers. She lifted a brooch of lacy gold adorned with shiny stones.

"This was my mama's pin. Papa gave it to me, too. But I could never wear it. Had to hide it away in the barn. With you—you can wear it—like it should be. And the watch—though you wouldn't wear it—can be displayed. I saw one once—in a little glass case—draped over blue velvet. It looked so beautiful."

The words puzzled Damaris, but she reached out her trembling hands to accept the two priceless gifts. If her mama had to hide them from her pa, how would they be safe with her? He never showed any reservation about entering her room to look for something he could exchange for money to purchase another bottle.

"But how—how can I—?" Damaris stammered, not knowing quite how to express her thoughts.

Her mama seemed to read her—as always. She pressed the gifts into the palms of her daughter's quivering hands and clasped them tightly in her own. Then she looked deep into the dark brown eyes.

"You are getting older, Damaris. Almost fifteen. And you

are tall for your age. Why—you could 'most pass for seventeen. At that age a lot of girls are—are on their own. Do you understand?"

Damaris wasn't sure she did, but she nodded her head.

"As to the gifts—keepin' them safe . . ." Mrs. Withers hesitated, still looking at Damaris. "You—you'll think of something," she finished in a whisper.

Damaris saw pain in her mother's pleading eyes. A tear spilled from one and ran down the pale cheek. Damaris had seldom seen her mama weep—even when her father yelled at her and hit her in a drunken rage.

Damaris reached down and tucked the little bundle in the pocket of her apron. She still wasn't sure what her mama expected of her, but she would do her best. Perhaps she could hide the treasures in one of the farthest corners of the attic. Her pa never seemed to notice the small trapdoor in the ceiling above her dresser. Perhaps the cherished items would be safe there.

She looked at her mama and nodded again. The woman was standing, brushing back strands of wayward hair, blinking tears from her eyes.

"We must get to bed," her mama said suddenly. "Must get some rest before he wakes. He might well be sick come mornin'."

Damaris knew her mother was right. Her pa was often sick when he woke up from his drinking. It could mean bedding to wash, floors to scrub, nursing to be done. Her mama would do the comforting and easing of the misery. Damaris would be assigned the scrubbing—of clothes, blankets and wooden boards.

She sighed as she moved to wash the cups. She and her mama would enjoy only a brief respite. They should make the most of it.

With one hand in her apron pocket holding fast the two treasures, Damaris climbed the creaking steps and made her way to her simple bed. Perhaps she could get a few hours of sound sleep before her pa wakened.

Chapter Two

A Daring Idea

Climbing up through the attic hole in the darkness would be too risky. Damaris would have to wait for the light of day before hiding the treasures Mama had given her. She was sure she would be up and about long before her pa cried out for a cold cloth for his forehead and a slop pail for his upset stomach.

Long into the night Damaris lay thinking, fingering beneath her pillow the tiny cloth bundle with the treasures that had once belonged to her grandparents. Damaris sighed and turned over. If only there was no money. If only her pa didn't make the trips into town to spend his time at the saloon tables. If only her mama didn't look so old and tired all of the time. If only—

Damaris checked herself. There was no use going on. Things were as they were. Nothing would change. Nothing. Damaris reached a hand up to feel the scar above her temple. At least her pa had thrown nothing at her—this time. He had not slapped her nor twisted her arm. They had gotten off easy this time—both her and her mama. Damaris was thankful for that. But what about next time? And the time after that? She lived in fear and dread of each new day, and she was sure her mama did likewise.

What if her pa awoke and found out that the two women-folk had been drinking his precious coffee? What if he discovered that an expensive-looking brooch had been hidden away from him for many years? What if he learned of the watch?

Damaris again slipped a hand under the pillow to feel the items. For a moment she felt a flash of anger toward her mama. Why had she given her these dangerous possessions? Was she too old and weary to continue hiding them herself?

Her mama had seemed so—so different tonight. Oh, she was still pale, still weary, but for just a moment she had let down her guard and shown the woman who used to be.

Damaris puzzled again over her mother's words. *Many girls of seventeen are on their own. You could pass for seventeen.* The strange message played and replayed through the young girl's mind. But she could make no sense of it.

There are choices we can make, the voice went on.

Choices? What choices. Not the color of one's eyes. Mama had made that clear enough. Then what choices?

Damaris had never had choices. If she could have chosen, she would be attending school like all of the other children in the neighborhood. But she couldn't choose. Her pa had done that for her when she reached the age of twelve.

"Yer ma needs ya," he had growled. "Ain't right fer you to be fritterin' away yer day when yer ma is home doin' all the chores. Girl big as you should be able to earn her keep."

So Damaris had been taken from school and put to work with the household and farm chores. It wasn't that she minded the work. She was big for her age and surprisingly strong, but she did hate to miss the classes. Now she had no access to books. Books and the adventure of learning. She missed school.

Damaris had never gone to the little church in town, but she longed to go. She envied the laughing, happy children dressed in their pretty frills and hair bows.

"Why don't we ever go to church?" she asked once.

Her mother shook her head sadly and looked down at the faded apron covering her worn dress with its many patches.

"Can't go to church like this," she responded.

Damaris knew that was so. She closed her mouth on further coaxing and pushed the thoughts from her mind for a time, but later in the day she couldn't resist pressing just a bit. She was hungry for information.

"Did you ever go to church?" she asked.

"Oh my, yes," her mother answered quickly, then cast a glance around to see if they were being heard. When sure they were alone, she continued. "I always went to church when I was a girl. Papa and Mama always took us. Every Sunday."

"Then you know about it. What is the black book they carry?"

"The black book? Why, that's the Bible, child."

"A Bible. Does it—does it have stories?"

For a moment her mother's eyes shadowed; then she said, "Child, it's a shame, it is, that you even have to ask. The—the Bible tells us about God. The stories are all about Him—and others. Many others. Some brave. Some kind. Some daring. Some—sinful. My pa used to read from the Bible every morning before I was allowed to leave the table."

Damaris felt envious. To be read a story every morning seemed almost too good to be true.

"Your name came from the Bible," her mama shocked her by saying.

"My name? It did?" Damaris felt her breath catch in her throat. Her name came from the black book.

"What does it—what does it say about me?" she asked in a whisper.

Her mama shook out another worn dishtowel and pegged it to the line. "I don't rightly remember," she said. "It was a long time ago thet I read the words. Just the name stayed with me."

Damaris found it hard to contain her excitement. "I wish we had a Bible," she sighed before she could check the words.

"I did—at one time," said her mother through tight lips.

"When?" Damaris asked. "What happened to it?"

"When I was a girl. I even had it when I got married, but a few years later yer pa needed—" She checked her words and shook out one of the worn dresses that belonged to her daughter.

"Did you have pretty dresses?" Damaris asked, looking at her own faded dress hanging limply on the line.

Her mama looked at the shabby garment and sighed. "Yes," she admitted softly, "I had pretty dresses."

Damaris was about to ask another question, but her mama gave her hand a little wave to dismiss the conversation and spoke almost sharply, "Now off with you. The hens are waiting for fresh water." Damaris ran to care for the hens, but her thoughts were still on the little white church, the black book with her name in it and pretty dresses.

She never again asked her mother about church, but she still wished she could join the carefree girls with their pretty frocks and discover for herself just what church was all about. But Damaris had no choice.

Are there really choices? Damaris wondered as she lay in the darkness. She had never known her mama to lie to her. What had she meant? Damaris shifted in her bed again. In the distance she heard her pa's snoring turn to groans. Was he waking already? Wouldn't they get the sleep they so badly needed? Damaris shut her eyes tightly against the blackness and willed herself to quit her troubled thinking and go to sleep while she had the opportunity.

But her thoughts would not be stilled.

Choices. Choices. Her brain kept hammering the word at her. What choices did she have? What choices did her mama have? They were trapped. Both of them. There was nothing they could do to free themselves.

If I had a choice, thought Damaris, *I wouldn't stay here. I'd go some place far away and—and work like mama said and—and buy a new dress and—and go to church and—and find my name in the Bible and read the story for myself.*

The sudden train of thought surprised Damaris. Never before had she even dared to think of going away. Now she couldn't dismiss the idea.

"I could," she admitted to herself in a shaky whisper. "I could. I really don't have to stay here. I—I am big enough to—to—"

The thought made Damaris shiver.

"I could. I could run away—to town. No, farther than that. Pa would find me there—for sure. I'd go—I'd go off down the road somewhere—somewhere far away—and I'd work for somebody. Hoeing gardens and milking cows or—doing the washing or something. I'd work hard. Then—" Damaris checked her thoughts. She must be careful. Extremely careful. If her pa had any idea that she was fostering such a wild and foolish notion, he would thrash her within an inch of her life. Damaris glanced at the stairs that led down from her little loft room, separating her from the living quarters and the bedroom below. She feared that her pa might even now be reading her thoughts—and spoiling her plan.

She must move carefully. She possessed very little, but she would need to bundle her few clothes. She would have to take her blanket. She might need to sleep in the open until she reached the far-off town. She would need to take a few slices of her mama's bread and perhaps a boiled egg or two— or a few pieces of cooked salted pork. She would need a bottle of some kind with some well water. She wouldn't be able to stop at farm homes on the way to ask for water because her pa would be able to track her if she dared to show herself. She needed to fix her worn shoes—somehow. They would never do for a long walk with the soles as worn as they were. And she must—must take the watch and brooch. She would sew them inside her garments or pin them in a pocket so that no thief would ever find them. Then, when she got where she was going, she would put the watch under glass on blue velvet, just as her mama had dreamed, and she would pin the brooch to the front of her dress and wear it to church every Sunday.

———

The next few days passed without incident. There was no money for a trip to town, so Mr. Withers spent his days working on the harness and puttering around the farmyard. He was almost pleasant when he had not been drinking, and Damaris even heard him whistle once or twice.

But toward the end of the week his need for liquor began

to tell on him again. Damaris could see it in his eyes and hear it in the agitation of his voice. Would he find money? Damaris was sure they had nothing more to trade for cold cash—except the horse or one of the cows. Damaris noticed her mother cast nervous glances toward the barn. She hoped her pa was not desperate enough to totally forfeit their future. As the days ticked slowly by, his eyes became more shifty and he often licked his lips as though they were parched and dry.

Damaris speeded up her own plans. She managed to find some heavy cardboard and borrowed her mama's sewing shears to cut insoles for her shoes.

She patched the three dresses she owned one more time and mended the tear in her apron.

She slipped her slice of dinner bread into her pocket. Later she wrapped it in brown paper and stashed it in her attic hiding place with the others she had been saving from each meal.

The next time her father rode off to town, she knew she must bundle her few belongings and slip through the woods that stood tall behind the farmyard. She dared not take the road for the first several miles lest she be seen by some of the neighbors.

It pained her that she would not dare tell her mama goodbye, but Damaris knew instinctively that the best parting gift she could give her mama was innocence. When her father questioned her whereabouts, her mama must be able to truthfully say she had no idea where their daughter was.

So Damaris watched and waited, biding her time, but carefully plotting her escape. She had been given a choice—a choice she had never expected to receive—and she knew she must seize the opportunity. Never again would she quiver with fright, wondering just what her pa might do in his drunken state.

Damaris stole quick glances at her mother as they worked side by side, scrubbing at the washboard, hoeing in the garden, caring for the farm hens, gathering eggs for bartering, wondering if she knew of her daughter's plan. But they worked in silence for the most part, each glad for a respite from Mr. Withers's drunkenness.

Then one day Damaris saw her pa slip into the chicken coop and stuff a pair of unwary fowl into a gunnysack. The urge for drink had gotten the better of him again.

Damaris watched her pa tie the gunnysack behind the saddle and hoist himself onto the back of old Rob. Without a glance toward the house he urged the horse down the lane and out onto the dusty road.

"He's going," Damaris said to her mama with anger, fear, and sadness all contained in her voice. "I saw him take two hens."

Her mama only nodded, but as she turned away Damaris thought she caught the glimmer of tears in her eyes. It puzzled her. Her mama was not one for crying—even when she was in pain.

Mrs. Withers cast a glance at the afternoon sky. The sun hung overhead, its warm rays beating down with strength.

"Two hens won't keep 'im long," she commented. Damaris nodded. Her pa was even more difficult when he went drinking and didn't get his fill.

"He might be back by suppertime," mused her mama, shading her eyes from the sun for a moment and then brushing the hair back from her face.

Damaris nodded again. For a moment she wavered. This didn't seem like the right time to be going. If her pa came home without his thirst fully quenched, he would be even more abusive than usual, and if she wasn't there, her mama might receive double share.

Next time, Damaris told herself, but her mama surprised her by cutting into her thoughts.

"I know how much you like wading in the crick, an' you haven't had a chance fer weeks now. Why don't you run on down an' have you a wade 'fore yer pa gits back from town."

Damaris felt a tremble go through her body. The creek was in the woods—behind the farmyard. It lay directly on the route that Damaris had planned to take.

"I think thet I'll jest lay down an' have myself a bit of a

nap. Didn't sleep too good last night," her mama went on. And so saying she moved toward the house. Damaris followed at her heels, still undecided as to what she should do.

"Just sorta tiptoe out when ya leave," the woman said. "My head is botherin' me some."

Damaris nodded and watched her mama enter her bedroom and shut the door.

The question seemed to have been decided for her then. There would never be a greater opportunity. Damaris urged herself up the stairs to the loft and quietly gathered her few belongings into her shawl. Then she stepped onto her bed, up onto the dresser, and carefully lifted aside the trapdoor. It was getting more and more difficult for her to hoist her body through the small opening. If she stayed, she wasn't sure how much longer she would have been able to use her secret place.

From the safety of the rafters she withdrew her pieces of bread and her cloth-wrapped treasures. With one final look around the dusty cavern that had been her sanctuary, Damaris eased herself back through the trapdoor, pulled the cover into place, and stepped to the bed, then to the floor.

With as little noise as possible she finished the task of binding everything together. Then she crept from the room without looking back.

As she passed the bedroom where her mother lay, she hesitated for one moment, listened to the silence, then sighed deeply and continued on tiptoe.

The kitchen door closed softly behind her. She walked across the porch, watching for the board that always creaked, took the steps in rapid order, and turned toward the woods.

She was on her way. She had made a choice and taken the first step on her own. She only wished with all of her heart that her mama was going with her.

Her heart pounded with the enormity of her daring. She had no idea what lay before her, nor how she would ever make her way in the new, strange world she was facing. She braced her shoulders and lifted her chin. At least now she was free to make her own choices.

Chapter Three

Travel

Damaris had only one thought—to put as many miles between herself and her farm home as quickly as she could. For that reason she walked briskly, not even stopping to test the waters of her beloved creek. She crossed on the fallen log thrown across for a walking bridge and hastened off on the other side, following the path that the milk cows had made on their way to the meadow beyond.

Damaris did not head for the meadow. Instead, she deserted the traveled path and struck a line directly through the trees. She would hit the back road if she calculated right. It was lightly traveled and would lead her directly away from the small town where her pa was headed.

The trees overhead formed some protection from the hot afternoon sun, and Damaris was thankful for the shade. But the day was stuffy-warm and it made her thirsty. She hated to drink so soon from her little bottle of precious well water. She had many miles to walk and didn't know when she might be able to replenish her supply.

In a short time she reached the rickety fence that marked off her pa's land and climbed through it with no difficulty. She wondered why the cows kept to the confines of the property. They could have made their escape just as easily if they ever had a mind to.

Damaris cast a cautious glance up and down the road before daring to show herself. Seeing no one, she carefully picked her way through the scrub brush and onto the dusty track.

For a moment she stood looking up and down the road, making sure that her trip through the trees had not disorientated her. What a calamity it would be if she found herself at Mr. Maynard's mercantile instead of in a town up the line.

But Damaris was sure of herself and stepped out confidently in the opposite direction of the town.

She would eventually need to get onto a more well-traveled road to find any kind of civilization. To find work she would need to be where there were people. But first she must put some distance between herself and the folks who knew her.

All through the heat of the afternoon she walked as briskly as her tired legs allowed. The holes in her shoes, even though covered with the cardboard, were bothering her feet. Damaris didn't know how much longer she would be able to carry on. Finally she stopped and slipped off the shoes, tied the laces together, and hung them over her shoulder. She was used to the feel of the hard-packed earth beneath her feet, and she reasoned that it would be more comfortable going barefoot than having the worn shoes slopping on her feet.

But the broken track was not kind to Damaris's feet, and it wasn't long until she was limping.

Still she must go on. She must. Her pa could easily ride that far and take her off home again. So she pressed forward, allowing herself a small sip now and then from her bottle of water.

It was getting dark before Damaris realized she had gone about as far as she could for the first day. She was still on the simple track, but she had no idea how far she had traveled. She had seen very few farms, and the road itself seemed to be petering out. She wondered if she would soon come to an impassable swamp or some other obstacle.

When she could hardly see, Damaris slowed her steps, and made her way toward the side of the road, looking about her to find some kind of shelter. She was thirsty, tired, and her feet felt as if they were on fire.

She eased herself onto a stump by the roadside and drew out her bottle. Two wee sips were all she allowed her parched throat. Then she unwrapped the little store of bread and lifted out one piece. It wasn't nearly enough to ease her hunger, but Damaris had left the table unsatisfied on more than one occasion so she was set to suffer a grumbling stomach now.

Finding a large tree with a canopy of spreading branches, she pushed her way under it until she pressed close to the trunk. Then she put down her shawl-wrapped bundle for a pillow, tucked her worn blanket closely about her, and eased herself to the ground. Damaris kicked her burning feet free of the blanket and extended them into the cool of the evening air.

She did not waste time lamenting. Did not even allow herself to wonder "What if. . . ?" She would need all her energy for the ordeal ahead. She was weary and it was late and she had to be up in the morning with the rising of the sun. She pulled the blanket more closely about her shoulders and shut her eyes. It would be good to sleep. Perhaps her stomach would even cease its complaining once sleep claimed her.

———

Damaris was up even before the sun made an appearance. She wanted a drink, but she decided to wait until she had traveled a good distance. The morning was cool, and she shivered as she bundled her things together and hoisted them to her shoulders. The warmth of the pack helped to ease the trembling of her body, and she struck off again.

For the first few miles she wore her shoes. The sun now was up and the day was already growing hot. She sipped from her bottle and allowed herself another half slice of the dried bread. Then the track she had been traveling disappeared into the hardness of the unplowed ground. She crossed several dusty roadways, but Damaris still didn't feel safe traveling on a proper road, so she angled across them, making her way farther and farther west.

By noon she was weary, hungry, and thirsty, but the water in her small bottle was gone. Although she could see on the distant hills the smoke from farm chimneys, she had no intention of going near a place where she might be identified.

Then a wondrous thing happened. Damaris saw a long stretch of raised ground she recognized as a railroad track—and it was heading in a westerly direction.

Her heart beat faster. The tracks would eventually lead to a town. Damaris mounted the rise and allowed herself a few minutes of rest before heading toward the point where the rails touched the skyline.

She hadn't gone far when the tracks crossed a small creek. Damaris ran forward toward the cool water and the chance to quench her thirst. She drank from the stream, refilled her water bottle, and then bathed her burning feet.

"I wonder if you are the same little crick that flows by our farm," she spoke to the stream. It was the first time she had used her voice since yesterday and it sounded strange to her in the stillness.

I s'pose not, she thought, but she did not speak again. She didn't like the feeling of emptiness around her when she spoke into the shimmering heat of the day.

As she soaked her feet she withdrew another half of a bread slice and ate it ever so slowly, drinking long and often between each bite. The water helped to ease the pain in her stomach as well as quench her thirst.

At last she was ready to travel on. Her feet felt somewhat better and she slipped her shoes on once more. She would wear them for as long as she could endure. They offered her feet at least a little protection from the rough stones.

Night was closing in around her before she stopped again. As darkness fell she could see lights in the distance. There were too many huddled together for it to be a farm, so she knew she was near a town. She wondered about its name and how many miles she had traveled from her home. Surely not enough. She would bypass the town, catch the tracks on the other side, and continue west. Perhaps in a few days she would feel safe enough to stop and look for work so she could eat properly again.

Damaris pulled the blanket tightly about her shoulders and rested her head on her shawl-pillow. She pulled her bottle of water under the blanket with her, knowing how important it was to her well-being. Then she closed her eyes and let her weary body be overtaken by sleep.

Damaris bypassed the town as planned, though it was difficult to keep her resolve. She wanted so much to see people, find a job, and eat a decent meal. Her stomach knotted with hunger, and the little pieces of dried bread did little to ease the pangs.

But Damaris knew she was not yet safe. She walked around the town, avoiding contact with anyone. Once she saw a boy out gathering the cows for milking. She wanted to ask if she could fill her small bottle with the fresh milk, but she had nothing to offer in return and she couldn't ask the boy to give up the milk with no payment.

She trudged on. It was late morning before she circled her way back to the train tracks. With despair she noted that now they were aiming more south than west. She squinted her eyes against the bright sun. In the distance she could see that they turned and headed west again. With thankfulness, she set out once more on her journey.

In the late afternoon she stopped suddenly, heart thumping, and shaded her eyes with her hand. Down the tracks, moving slowly toward her, was a single walker. Damaris didn't know whether to dash for the safety of trees or to continue on her way. But only cleared fields lined the railway. The trees were far in the distance. To try to take cover would cost her too much time. Besides, surely the walker had already seen her. If he wanted to rob her he could follow her into the woods. She had often met neighborhood men on her errands to town and none had ever bothered her, but what would keep a stranger from harming her, especially in this desolate place?

But then another alarming thought occurred to her. What if he wasn't a stranger? If he recognized her, he would surely tell her father where he had seen her. She frantically hoped this man *was* a total stranger.

Unable to come up with a plan other than a direct meeting with the walker, Damaris plodded on.

She kept her eyes lowered, watching each place that she set her foot. Now and then she stole a brief glance upward. The man was near enough for her to see his features now. He was a stranger.

Damaris continued. She squared her shoulders and tried to look less tired. She didn't want the man to guess how far she really had come, how weary she really was. She wanted him to think she could outrun him if she had to. He was heading east. There was a chance—just a chance—that when he passed through the next town he might mention he had met a strange young girl along the railroad tracks. Damaris was thankful that her own small town had no access to train travel. These tracks would not lead him there.

Strengthening her resolve, Damaris kept walking toward the stranger. As they neared each other their eyes met for a moment. Damaris was surprised to see that the stranger was dressed even more shabbily than she. He looked tired and gaunt. For a moment she considered giving him the few chunks of stale bread still in her possession.

But he dropped his gaze again and walked by her without so much as a nod of acknowledgment. Damaris felt both relief and disappointment. She trudged on, turning to look back at him only once.

She did not reach another town that day. At night she bundled up again and slept close to the tracks. There were storm clouds in the distance, and she feared she might be wakened by rain in her face. She decided to get as much sleep as she could before the storm broke upon her.

Chapter Four

Town

The rain didn't start until the next morning. Damaris was already on her way down the railroad tracks when the first drops fell. She debated whether to keep on walking or take shelter. She had walked in rain before and did not mind it, but she knew the things she carried would be soaked if she did not find some place to tuck them away. When a grove of trees not far to her left came into view, Damaris ran for it. Her eyes looked back to the storm clouds. She hoped there would be no lightning or she wouldn't be safe under the trees. The storm was not a thunder shower, so Damaris crept as close to the trunk of a big tree as she could. She tucked her belongings beneath her skirts, hoping to keep them dry.

"I hope it doesn't last long," she murmured.

Then she reached for her supply of bread and water. She might as well refresh herself as she waited. Maybe she would even be able to sleep.

She allowed herself half a slice of bread and drank sparingly of the water, not knowing when she might be able to fill her water bottle again. She looked with longing at the emptying sky. If only she had some way to fill her bottle from all the water falling around her.

The air grew cool. Damaris wrapped her blanket around her shoulders and tried to get some rest, but sleep would not come. For the first time since starting her journey, she allowed her thoughts to return to home.

How was her mama? Had she been surprised when Damaris failed to return from wading in the crick? Had she gone looking for her thinking she might have fallen and drowned or broken a leg or some such thing? Had her pa been terribly angry when she didn't respond to his call? Damaris hoped with all of her heart that he hadn't taken it out on her mama.

In the distance a whistle blew. For a moment Damaris's thoughts scrambled to identify the sound. At last she recognized it as a train whistle and tipped her head to listen for the sound to be repeated.

"Here I been followin' the tracks fer miles," she chided herself, "an' I don't even recognize a train whistle when I hear one."

The whistle blew again, closer now, and Damaris could not resist creeping out from the tree to watch the train pass.

"Sure don't run very often," she mused. "I been on thet track fer two days an' this is the first train I've seen."

The train was heading west, and how Damaris wished she was on board.

"If I had the ticket money, I'd be off out of here in a flash," she reasoned. "No more walking with blistered feet, no more hiding from the rain. Just think, I could be where I want to go in next to no time."

But Damaris did not have the money for a ticket, so there was no use wasting time and energy longing for it. She huddled back under her blanket again and willed the rain to stop.

But it didn't stop. It continued to pelt straight down from the heavens.

"At least the wind's not blowing," Damaris observed with relief. "Even these trees wouldn't protect me if it was windy."

She was so weary. Surely she could sleep if only her stomach wasn't tormenting her so. She pulled the blanket closely about her and arranged her little bundle behind her head. At last she managed to drop off to sleep, but not for long. Her stomach wouldn't let her.

It was almost dark before she allowed herself to reach for

her dwindling store of bread. Even though her supply was getting low, she had to have some nourishment. She finished her water. Surely with all of that rain she could find a stream where she could refill the bottle. She had to have rest, and she couldn't sleep with her stomach so empty. Damaris knew as she looked out at the dripping world that she wouldn't be traveling for several hours. She ate all but one small slice of bread.

It was late the next afternoon before Damaris reached a small town. *I'm gonna have to stop here,* she told herself. *I need to find some work so I can eat.*

At the first house along the rutted road a woman was in the yard hanging up some washing. Damaris approached slowly, trying not to let her eagerness show.

"Good afternoon, ma'am," she began. Her voice sounded strange to her own ears. The woman looked up and squinted into the brightness of the sun.

"Don't think I know ya," she responded, but with no threat in her tone.

"No, ma'am. I'm—I'm just passing through. On my way—my way west."

The woman's frown deepened. Damaris read her suspicion. *She's gonna start asking questions,* Damaris thought, *and what am I gonna answer?*

Before the woman could open her mouth again, Damaris plunged ahead. "I'd be happy to lend a hand with the washin'."

Now the woman's head came up and she looked hard at Damaris.

"Don't know why a young girl like yerself would be wantin' to dirty her hands with my wash," she answered frankly. "Lest of course she had herself a good reason. You're not runnin' away from home, are ya, girl?"

Damaris was stunned by her astuteness. She hardly knew how to respond. She lifted her head, making her stubborn chin protrude.

"I'm on my own, ma'am," she said, knowing that much was true. Then she continued, mixing truth with as little error as possible. "Mama says thet a girl of seventeen should be able to work her way."

Her mama had made the remark. If the woman chose to believe Damaris was seventeen, the error would be hers. She hadn't told an outright lie.

But the woman still looked doubtful. "Guess I can manage my own wash," she said simply. "I'm 'most done anyhow."

Damaris nodded her head in dejected acknowledgment, bid the woman a good-day, and continued down the road.

Her next attempt was at a home where a woman worked with a hoe. Beads of perspiration stood out on her forehead and she stopped now and then to place a hand on her back.

She needs help and that's for sure, thought Damaris, determined not to lose out again. This time she needed to have some answers ready. But Damaris did not have time to get it all worked out. She had already reached the woman.

"Afternoon, ma'am." She tried to keep the fear and uncertainty from her voice.

The woman looked up, lifted a large hanky from her apron pocket, and mopped her brow.

"Looks like you got a fair ways to hoe yet," observed Damaris.

The woman nodded.

"I have a bit of time," continued Damaris, "and I don't mind hoeing. Mama used to say that I had a good back for it. 'Course that was before I lost my mama."

The woman didn't comment, and Damaris took heart. She had not been dismissed.

"I'm on my way to an aunt now," continued Damaris, "now that I—I don't have a home of my own." She hesitated to let the words sink in. The woman still did not respond. *Is she deaf?* Damaris wondered.

"I need a bit of a break from my walkin'. I'd be happy to hoe for a spell."

"What ya charge?" the woman finally asked.

Damaris heaved a sigh. The woman had understood her well enough.

"Just a place to sleep the night and a few supplies for the journey," she answered.

"I don't have no extry bed," the woman stated.

"Then the supplies will do," Damaris said quickly.

The woman didn't look particularly pleased with the arrangement, but Damaris could see she was mighty tired of hoeing in the hot sun.

Damaris waited patiently as the woman made up her mind. At last she passed the hoe to Damaris. "I'll give ya yer supper—nothin' more."

Damaris nodded. It was a hard bargain but she was not in the position to turn it down.

She laid aside her bundle and took the hoe. She had hoped a meal might come first, but apparently the woman didn't want to part with food until she was sure the stranger kept her part of the bargain.

Damaris began to make her way down the row, and the woman, after watching for a few minutes to be sure Damaris knew what she was doing, mopped her brow again and turned toward the house.

"Please, ma'am," called Damaris, "would you mind if I had a drink. I've run out of water."

The woman turned and nodded toward the well in the yard. "Help yerself," she responded and continued on her way.

Damaris drank until she gurgled. It felt good to have her stomach full, if only with water. Then she turned back to her hoeing. She had a long way to go to earn her supper.

As Damaris worked, more than her stomach pained her. Her mother's training meant that her conscience made her as miserable as her emptiness. Her lies might have worked to get her a job, but she knew it was wrong to lie. Right there and then she made up her mind that she would not resort to falsehood again—not even if she starved as a result.

Supper was scant and served to Damaris on the porch. The woman seemed afraid to let her in the house. Damaris had hoped for enough food that she might tuck some away in her little cloth bundle for the future, but there was barely enough to satisfy her hunger. Besides, it was a watery stew that Damaris had no way of carrying.

She sopped up the last of the stew with bread that had been provided, thanked the woman, and rose from the porch. The woman did not even thank Damaris for her service.

It was beginning to get dark and Damaris had to find shelter for the night. It would not do to lie in the open in town as she had done along the empty railroad tracks.

It took some time for her to find a small shed that seemed to be deserted. It was musty and dirty, but Damaris knew she needed to settle herself for the night. She placed her bundle under her head, wrapped the blanket tightly around herself, and curled up to sleep. She was in a town. Her bruised and blistered feet would have a chance to heal. Her back, though weary and aching, should be rested by morning. Surely she could find work to support her before long. She would just keep looking until she did. In the meantime, she was dry, comfortably warm, and—she hoped—safe. And she could get water at one of the many nearby wells. She had put enough miles between her and her hometown that no one should recognize her, and she didn't think that her pa, no matter how angry he was over her leaving, would expend the energy to search this far for her.

Damaris felt reasonably safe as she curled up on the floor of the shed and shut her eyes in sleep.

———

During the following few days Damaris found little jobs here and there in the town, but nothing that really improved her situation. Each day she was pressed to find enough employment to guarantee her one decent meal. She was lucky once or twice. One woman had offered her a pair of shoes. They were worn and didn't fit well, but they were much better than the ones she had been wearing. Another lady allowed her to sleep in a shed at the back of her property. This gave Damaris a home of sorts, but she knew she would need to do much better before winter came.

Each day she made her rounds. Sweeping out a store, scrubbing floors, or pulling weeds. Once she was hired by the same woman for three whole days to do cleaning chores. But when the three days were up, she had nothing to show for it. She had been given only meals while she worked.

And then little trickles of gossip began to reach her ears. Folks were wondering who she was and where she had come from. Damaris knew she must move on. One morning, just as the sun peeked over the eastern horizon, Damaris rolled her belongings into a neat bundle and started off down the tracks.

She was into her second day before she arrived at the next small town. It was a welcomed sight, as she'd had nothing to eat since she worked for her last meal. She was bolder now—and her story, true as far as it went, was more rehearsed. She lost no time seeking out a small job in exchange for something to eat.

The first woman gave her a flat no and an icy look, but Damaris was not easily discouraged. Her very existence depended upon her finding some job that would return her with a meal—even if only a piece of bread.

Doggedly she moved from house to house. On her fifth try she was told there was ironing to do.

The woman looked kindly at her, noting her dirty, mended dress and worn shoes.

"Come in, dear," she said without hesitation. "I can use a little help—providing your wages aren't too high."

"Just a place to rest and a bit to eat," answered Damaris, not wanting to be turned away again.

"Sit down," said the woman, ushering Damaris into her tidy kitchen. "We have just finished our own meal. I think the food is still warm enough."

Damaris was not worried about a *warm* meal. She needed sustenance.

The woman heaped a plate with vegetables and a slice of ham, then placed two biscuits on the side and handed the plate to Damaris. The famished girl found it hard to remember the few manners her mama had taught her. She wanted to devour the food and tuck away what was left before the woman had a chance to change her mind.

The food made Damaris sleepy. She had eaten too much, too quickly, and her stomach complained as she took her place at the ironing board. By sheer willpower she kept her head up and her body moving. From clothes basket to stove to ironing board she went, working her way through the warm afternoon.

When supper was finally announced, Damaris was hanging the last white shirt on a hanger.

"My husband is the town doctor," the woman informed her. "That's why I always have such a big ironing. Folks just take it for granted that he will have a clean shirt every day. Sometimes two or three a day—depending on his circumstances."

Damaris nodded.

"You must be weary," the woman continued. "That was a big job—and such a warm afternoon, too. The doctor will soon be home and we'll have our supper."

Damaris had smelled the meal cooking as she worked and was surprised that she could feel hungry again, considering what she had eaten only hours before.

"There he is now," said the woman as the back door opened and closed. "Come now. We'll eat right away. The doctor will be starving."

Damaris stood where she was. "Please, ma'am," she faltered. "If it's the same to you—could I—could I take my plate on the back porch?"

The woman turned mid-step to look at the girl. "My! You are hot and weary, aren't you. Well, it is cooler out there, I'll grant you that. It always warms the house so with the stove burning. Of course. Take your plate to the porch."

Damaris let her eyes fall to her dress. She had washed it before leaving the previous town, but though clean, it was not fit for the parlor of a doctor and his wife.

The woman passed Damaris a large plate, then bustled about her kitchen getting her meal ready.

"You just help yourself. There's plenty here. And cold buttermilk or lemonade in the icebox," she said.

Damaris dished up her plate of food. This time she was more cautious. She did not wish to have her stomach ache from being too full any more than she wished to have it ache because it was too empty. She placed an ample serving on the plate, told herself that was the limit, and moved to the porch to enjoy the repast.

Chapter Five

An Opportunity

Damaris did not want to take advantage of the woman's kindness, so after she had washed the supper dishes she decided she should move on.

"Do you have a place to stay?" the woman asked.

"Oh yes," Damaris assured her, not bothering to mention that she would stay wherever she found a roof over her head.

"Well, if you must be going let me give you your wage."

"But I asked only my meals," put in Damaris.

"You worked much harder than that," said the woman as she fished around in a small dish in the cupboard. She came up with four coins and handed them to Damaris.

Damaris smiled her thank you and wished she hadn't been so hasty in making up her mind to leave. The woman might have found her other jobs to do. But the die was cast. Damaris shouldered her bundle and moved toward the door.

As she left the kitchen, Damaris noticed a black book lying on a small shelf. She paused, wishing again she could change her mind about leaving.

Here was a Bible. She was sure it was a Bible. Perhaps this kind woman would be able to tell her about her name.

"Thank you again for your help," the woman was saying. "I usually get my ironing done the first of the week, but we had a man here who needed nursing care. We don't have a nurse so I had to give a hand. He's on the mend now—so I should be able to keep up again."

Damaris nodded and moved again toward the door. She said goodbye and started down the street, casting her eyes back and forth as she went, wondering what other jobs might be available in this little town. She needed something more settled. Going from small task to small task would never meet her needs.

She would take one day at a time, she decided, and the first order of business was to find some place to sleep.

———

After Damaris had been in the town for three days, working here and there as she found someone to hire her, she started to hear excited chatter. She had no idea what the folks were talking about until she heard two elderly gentleman discuss the event as they sat in front of the hardware store. She drew near as she swept so she could hear their words.

"Not many trains go through here anymore," one man said.

His statement confused Damaris. She had seen two trains use the tracks just since she had been in town.

"Not many trains go through anywhere anymore," added the other old-timer. "I remember me a time when they went through three or four times a month in good weather."

The old fellow with the drooping gray mustache nodded in agreement.

"Guess a lot of folks take the rails now," he said, then spit at the ground.

"Hear it's expensive—iffen ya want to ship out all yer goods an' such," said the man in the stained straw hat.

"Yeah. Costly. But then everything costs yer shirt now."

"Yeah. Yeah," said the stained-straw-hat fellow.

"Anybody goin' from here?"

"Got two families goin' from what I hear. Thet new man and his brood. What's his name agin? Black? White? I never can remember."

"Brown?"

"Yeah—thet's the one. He's goin', and then thet young

fella—Travis. He an' his bride are goin'."

The two old men were silent for a few moments and Damaris was afraid she would have to move on. She had swept in one place far too long.

"I'd go myself—iffen I was younger. Shoulda done it years ago. Always had me a hankerin' to see the West. But you know the Missus. She wasn't anxious to pull up stakes and drag all the young'uns way out there. Kept talkin' 'bout school an' church an' doctorin'. Guess the West's got none of those things."

"Has now. Or so I heerd. Though I guess ya got to pick and choose the place ya head fer."

"Where's this train goin'?"

"Dunno. Ain't heard a name put to it."

Damaris had to move on, but as she eased herself away she heard one last statement that made her eyes lift up from the dust at her feet.

"Kinda sad," said the one with the gray mustache. "Kinda hate to see it come to an end. I know the rails are faster—an' I guess easier travelin'—but I'll miss seein' the wagon trains a passin' through. Always an air of adventure with the rumblin' of the wheels and the crackin' of the whips."

Damaris sucked in her breath. *A wagon train coming through town. A wagon train traveling west.* If only—if only she could join it. She would never again need to fear being found by her pa.

She wanted to ask the old gentlemen some questions, but she knew better than to approach them. She would just have to be alert—and ready. She would work her way west. Surely there were jobs she could do to earn her passage. Damaris could hardly contain her excitement as she went back into the store to replace the broom on the nail and collect her few cents of wages.

After asking several people, Damaris finally found out who was in charge of the wagon train. She approached the big man with some hesitation and spoke softly.

"Please, mister, could I speak with you a moment?"

Never before had she dared to address a man other than the store owner back home where she traded the farm eggs for a few groceries. Since being on the trail, she had always appealed to women for work. It took all of the courage she could muster to draw near to the man and ask for his attention.

He gave it reluctantly, lifting his head from the harness he had flung across his knees. His eyes did not soften as they took in the young girl before him, and he did not bother to answer her question. He just nodded his head in one quick, impatient motion, then turned his eyes back to the harness.

"I—I understand you are the wagon master," Damaris continued.

He nodded again without looking at Damaris.

She took a deep breath, glad that his eyes were not on her.

"I—I would like—would like passage west," she said hurriedly.

His head jerked up. "You got a team an' wagon?" he asked.

"No—o," answered Damaris, squirming before his stare.

"Don't take passengers. Check with the railroad train iffen ya want to travel west."

"But I thought—I mean—well, I—I thought—I don't have money for the fare."

"Then the answer is still no." He turned back to his work again.

"But I—I am more than willin' to work my way, sir," Damaris continued.

"Doin' what?"

"Why—why most anything. Cook. Wash. Herd. Anything."

"I do thet myself."

"But isn't there—I mean isn't there anything that I could do—for—for anyone?"

"Not thet I know of." His answer was sharp and blunt.

"Could I—could I ask?" she insisted. "You have several

wagons in your train. Maybe one of them could use—"

"Look, girlie," he said, his voice revealing irritation. "I have enough to take my attention 'thout setting out to care for a young girl who should be at home with her mama. I ain't in the least inclined to let you go 'round from wagon to wagon seein' iffen ya can bargain yer way fer a free trip. Now I think thet I've given more than thet minute you asked fer an' I've a heap of work to do, so iffen ya don't mind I'd like to git to it."

"Of—of course. I—I thank you kindly for your time," murmured Damaris. With her shoulders sagging and her eyes to the ground, she moved away from the man and his harness.

"Excuse me, miss," said a voice beside her. Damaris jumped with the suddenness of it. She had not seen the man approach her.

"Sorry," he apologized, "I didn't mean to startle you—but I couldn't help hearing your conversation with the captain."

Damaris waited, her eyes studying the stranger.

"I'm Mel Brown. Me and my wife an' family are joinin' this train. Now we got a passel of little folks, and I know the trip will be hard on my missus. Jest what kind of arrangement were ya fixin' to make?"

"Well, I—I just want—want to travel with the train. I—I have no money for fare, but I would work my way—just for the—the trip—and my meals. I—I'm fairly handy at household chores and I—I'm not afraid of work. My mama always said that I have a strong back and—"

The man raised his hand to bring her hurried words to an end.

"Where ya aimin' to go?" the man asked, catching Damaris off guard. She didn't even know the name of any western towns, and she hadn't heard anyone say where the train was heading.

"Same place you are," she answered dumbly, and the man accepted her answer without further pressing.

"Come," he bid her. "Talk to the Missus."

Damaris followed along behind him as they weaved in

and out among the tethered wagons.

At last they reached a covered wagon somewhat apart from the others. Damaris heard a baby crying and another young child whimpering for Mama. The man moved to the rear of the wagon, lifted the canvas flap, and called, "Martha."

An answer came from within and a woman soon stuck her head from the entrance. The crying baby was in her arms, and the demanding youngster was holding fast to the woman's skirts.

"This here young girl wants to travel west. Says she'll work her way along in exchange for the ride. Ya interested?"

The woman studied Damaris from top to bottom. There were questions in her eyes but she did not voice them. At length she nodded. She already looked tired and the trip had not yet begun.

"You'll ride in thet second wagon," she informed Damaris. "Our oldest boy is drivin' and there are three more young'uns in there. It'll be yer job to care fer 'em when we are on the move. When we stop ya can busy yerself with helpin' get the meals an' sech."

Damaris nodded.

"Put yer things in the wagon there an' gather some wood fer a fire. We'll need to eat before we set off, an' we don't have long to be fixin' it."

Damaris nodded again. She moved toward the wagon indicated and hoisted her small bundle of possessions under the canvas. Then she thought better of what she had done and climbed in after her load. She carefully untied the bundle and extracted the smaller packet that contained the watch and the brooch. Slipping it into her apron pocket, she fastened it shut with a pin from the hem of her dress. Then she climbed back down from the wagon and made her way to the small grove of trees clustered beside the road. Mrs. Brown had asked her to bring wood for a fire. She would hasten to carry out her first assignment lest the woman change her mind and leave her behind.

Damaris hurried with the wood and soon had a fire going.

She picked up the two available buckets and headed for one of the town wells. As soon as she was back she took a large kettle from the side of the wagon and put water on to heat. Then she went to the wagon entrance and called to the woman that she was ready to begin meal preparations if she could be given her instructions.

It was a simple meal that Damaris prepared but no one complained about it, and after she hurried to wash up the dishes and pack them away for the trip she saw a look of relief on the woman's face.

"I need to nurse this one," the woman said, lifting the baby and rising from the stool where she sat. "Thet one needs a nap iffen ya can coax him to settle," and she nodded her head at the boy who had been crying and hanging on to his mother's skirts ever since Damaris first saw him.

Damaris had misgivings as she picked up the young tot and headed for the wagon she had been told was hers to share. He screamed for his mother, but Damaris continued walking.

She knew very little about caring for children. That was one chore she had never done, having had no siblings of her own. Her reasoning told her, however, that if the child was to be settled for a nap, he first had to be comforted, so when she reached the wagon she crawled aboard and began to gently rock the little one in her arms, singing a song that her mama used to sing to her.

He continued to scream for a while, but gradually the wild complaining ceased. Damaris continued to rock, continued to sing. She rocked until her arms ached and sang until her throat was dry. At long last the child fell asleep and Damaris moved to gently lay him on the blanket bed that covered almost the entire wagon floor.

He stirred and started to whimper as she lowered him, and Damaris feared she would need to begin all over again. She wasn't much taken with her role as nursemaid and figured she would more than earn her keep on the trip west if it meant caring for this wailing child the whole way. And according to the woman, there were three more somewhere.

Damaris had been much too busy over the dinner hour to be bothered with counting noses. Now, she supposed that it was her job to round up the rest. From the talk around the fire she knew the train would soon move on, leaving the small town behind.

Chapter Six

On the Trail

The days on the trail were not easy ones for Damaris. Besides hauling water, finding fuel for the fire, and helping with the meals and washing, she was put in charge of four children, including three girls who were independent and unruly. The youngest child, two-year-old Edgar, quickly changed from fighting her to clinging to her. Every move Damaris made he was either hanging on her or demanding to be carried. Damaris gathered sticks for the fire with Edgar hoisted on her left hip, hauled water from the stream with Edgar trailing on her skirts, cooked the dinner over the fire with Edgar crying at her elbow. Damaris soon yearned for a few moments by herself—but they never came.

Even at night there was no escape, for she had to share the wagon—and her bed—with Edgar and his three sisters. Damaris felt as if she were smothering and often climbed from the wagon in the middle of the night to find a few quiet moments walking in the darkness, even though the captain had forbidden anyone to leave the wagons at night.

The oldest boy, younger than Damaris, was sullen and sober and far too tired at the end of each busy day to cause any problem for her. They were two weeks on the trail before Damaris even learned his name, and then it was quite by accident.

Two of the girls, Nina and Trudy, were arguing over whose turn it was to ride on the wagon seat. After a lively spat that solved nothing, Nina turned to Trudy and screamed at the top of her voice, "It is too my turn! You just ask Conrad!" But when the case was taken to Conrad for appeal, he shrugged thin shoulders and spoke not a word. The squabble ended in a hair-pulling match, and Damaris had to intervene. She stated firmly that both girls would miss their turn for the day and that made the quarrel turn against her, as the two fighting sisters suddenly found a common foe and banded together to give Damaris a piece of their angry minds.

If Damaris had looked forward to the excitement of the trip, she would have been disillusioned. There was nothing exciting about the long, hot, dusty trail they traveled. Nor in the long hours of difficult work. Each day started before sunrise and ended after the sun had sunk into the western sky.

If Edgar slept well, she could get a good six hours of sleep, but that was not always so. If he awakened in the night, the first thing he did was reach for her. If he didn't find her within grasping distance, he began to howl before he even had his eyes open.

I promised to earn my way, Damaris reminded herself daily, *and I will keep my word.*

Damaris really didn't have too much contact with her lady employer. Once her duties had been assigned and assumed, the woman withdrew to her wagon and appeared only when the next meal was ready. She didn't seem to be too well, and the small baby she always had in her arms was terribly fussy.

"Don't know iffen it's the heat or the constant motion," the exhausted woman said to Damaris one day, "but he sure isn't takin' to somethin'."

Damaris nodded in agreement, though she knew nothing about small babies.

———

Damaris had never known that so many miles of nothingness could exist. They saw hills and scrub brush and an occasional deer or coyote. Barren plains shimmered in heat waves, making Damaris feel dizzy and sick to her stomach. Now and then a thunder shower burst upon them, making everyone take cover in the moving wagons. If it rained too much the wagons were forced to sit a spell. Damaris hated these stops, for every delay meant more days on the trail.

She lost all track of time—but she guessed it really didn't matter which day of the week it was. Day after tiresome day was much like the other.

Damaris did not mix with the other families of the train. She had spotted one girl about her age, but the girl seemed totally free of responsibility and able to run about with the younger children. She even had a pony she rode whenever she felt so inclined. The rest of her time she spent curled up on pillows in the back of their wagon, a book propped up on her knees.

Damaris envied the girl. She didn't care that much about having no chores to do. She wasn't even too concerned about the pony, but the books made Damaris jealous. Oh, what she would give to be able to sit and read and read. She had had to leave her own worn volumes behind. They really were her mother's books, and Damaris hadn't felt right about taking them with her—but oh, it was hard to leave them.

After the evening meal had been served, the dishes washed and put up for the night, the water hauled for morning, and enough wood stacked to supply the breakfast fire, Damaris sometimes had a few moments before she tucked herself into bed.

They were not really free moments, for Edgar refused to go to bed without her, but Damaris often picked up the small boy and carried him as she wound her way around the campsite.

She would watch people gathered in little clusters, talking around this or that campfire. Sometimes she drew close enough to catch bits and pieces of the conversation. She wanted to learn how many more days they would be on the trail and if the tiresome journey was ever to end.

She avoided the menfolk, especially the wagon master.

For the first few days of the journey she was terrified that he would send her back to the town where she had joined the train if he discovered her.

About the third day he finally saw her, but he said nothing, just scowled, nodded, then passed her by. Damaris breathed a relieved sigh. She was safe. She could continue her trip west.

Still, Damaris chose to stay well out of his way, not wishing to bother him or cross him.

One thing about the journey pleased Damaris. There were no towns—and no saloons. Never once on the whole trail did Damaris see a drunken man. Never once did she see a woman or child bearing cuts or bruises because of someone's fit of drunken rage. Damaris, as eager as she was to reach a town, also dreaded the thought, sure that once they arrived the men would return to their normal way of life.

"If nothin' slows us, we should be there in three days."

The words had been spoken by a tall man resting against the wheel of his wagon.

Damaris, passing by with two buckets of water and Edgar clutching her skirt, caught her breath.

Three days! Only three more days. It sounded like a release from a moving prison.

The whole camp was abuzz that evening. Damaris even heard some singing. She ached to creep close and listen to the revelers, but her duties kept her near the fire. By the time she finished her chores, the music had stopped.

Damaris was too excited to sleep well that night. The flap of the wagon had been turned back to allow a little cool air to enter, and through the opening she could see the moon hanging silvery overhead. She could stand it no longer. She eased herself out from under the blankets, slipped her dress over her head, grabbed her shawl, and left the wagon. Edgar did not stir.

The captain's rule was that no one was to stray from the camp, by night or by day. But if they were close to a town,

Damaris reasoned, there should be no danger. Besides, she would not go far.

She crept past the other wagons and followed the small stream for a short distance. Then she sat down on a large rock by its shore and sighed, taking a deep breath of the clear night air.

In just three more days she would be out West. She would be free to settle in a new town, forget her short but troubled past, and make a new life for herself.

Her thoughts turned homeward. Instead of pushing them aside, she let them linger on her mama. For a moment Damaris had a difficult time recalling the well-loved face, and it frightened her. But soon the features came clearly to view and tears began to trickle down the girl's cheeks—the first tears she had allowed herself.

She wished there were some way to let her mama know she was doing just fine. More than that, she wished her mama was with her. She hoped with all of her heart that her mama was well.

Suddenly Damaris felt her chest tighten with fright. What if her going had caused Pa to beat Mama? What if she'd—? A deep sense of guilt seized Damaris. If Mama was in trouble it would be her fault. Her pa always became even more angry if his daughter wasn't there when he called. She had been selfish! She had been wrong to leave with no consideration for the only person who had ever loved her.

Now the tears fell freely. Damaris wiped them with her shawl and lifted her head to look toward the east. There was no way back. Perhaps there were wagons that traveled that way, but she had never heard of one. It would take her years and years to save enough money for train fare. By then her mama could be dead. She cried some more. And with her fright and guilt came a terrible wave of lonesomeness. Damaris would have given anything to be back home in her saggy cot in the small loft, listening to the snoring and groaning of her drunken father as the sounds ascended from below.

Finally Damaris got her tears under control but the ache within her did not go away. She watched the silent water ripple in the moonlight. The night was quiet and clear. Countless stars were visible overhead.

The sound of a step behind her brought her head up with a jerk.

Indians! was her first thought, and her whole body prepared itself to flee.

Damaris turned quickly to view the intruder and saw the wagon master standing a scant five feet behind her. She caught her breath, knowing she had broken the rule—the one, unchanging, indisputable order of the captain. She had left the train. Alone.

She was sure he would sentence her to immediate and terrible consequences. Should she dart and run or sit meekly and face his wrath? The latter had always worked best in the past. Only once had she tried to dodge under her pa's arm and avoid the punishment he had in mind. The beating she received that time was the worst one of her entire life. She had never tried it again.

Now she sat silently, appearing calm, but quivering inside.

The man moved closer and Damaris steeled herself for the blow that was to come. To her surprise his hand did not raise to strike her. Instead, he lowered himself to a rock a short distance away. Damaris heard his heavy sigh of contentment—or tiredness—she wasn't sure which. Still she did not move or speak.

"Pretty, ain't it?" he said after some moments of silence.

Damaris finally dared look at him.

He was taking in the expanse of sparkling night sky, looking quite relaxed, sharing her stream and her moonlight.

"Ya been pretty busy on this trip," he observed.

Damaris hadn't been aware that he had even noticed her.

After a few more minutes of silence he chuckled.

She lifted her head, still not sure if the man was being friendly or cruelly prolonging her agony.

"Thet there little fella sure don't let ya outta his sight, does he? Hangs on like you was a dog an' he was a flea." He laughed, and Damaris felt a smile curling the ends of her own mouth.

"Ya enjoy yer night walks, don't ya?"

Damaris quickly lost her smile and caught her breath. Now the punishment was coming.

"Well, I guess they haven't hurt nothin'. You've never strayed too far afield and with thet young'un hangin' on to you all the time—guess I don't blame ya none."

Damaris let out her breath. Not only had he discovered her tonight but apparently had observed her walks in the past. Why hadn't he said something before?

" 'Sides," he went on with a glance toward Damaris, "I had my eye on ya."

Damaris gathered the shawl more closely about her. It offered little protection from a beating but it was all she had.

"I decided right from the start thet as long as you stayed close an' caused no harm, I'd allow ya those little pieces of alone time. Couldn't bear to be so shut in like you been all the time. Couldn't bear it."

Damaris could not believe her ears. Did she understand him correctly? Was there to be no punishment? Had he actually allowed her to break his one steadfast rule? Before she had a chance to sort it all out, he changed the subject.

"We get to Poplar Creek in about three days," he said. "Is thet where yer aimin' for?"

Damaris nodded her head, hoping he could see her clearly enough in the moonlight to receive her answer.

"Not a bad little town—as western towns go. Quite small. Not too much work there fer a young girl, I expect, but ya might find somethin'."

Damaris listened closely.

"Don't s'pose ya want to go on workin' fer yer board and room carin' fer those Brown youngsters."

"No," said Damaris shaking her head. It was the first word she had spoken, and its forcefulness startled her.

He chuckled again and this time Damaris enjoyed the sound.

"Don't blame ya none," he said. "What kind of work are ya looking fer?" he asked.

Damaris hadn't given it much thought.

"I—I don't really know. 'Bout anything—for now. Later—later I'd like to do something—well, something like sewin' or—teachin' or something."

He nodded.

"Well, I know a few folks in town—not many, 'cause I never stop there fer long—but I might put in a word fer ya here or there. Not many girls yer age could outwork ya—I've seen thet firsthand."

Damaris knew she had been paid tribute. She lowered her head in embarrassment. She was not used to receiving compliments for completing assigned tasks.

He stood then and stretched his arms as though to work some kinks from his body.

"Well," he said, "guess it's 'bout time we both get back to our wagons. Sun's gonna be up before we know it."

Damaris rose from the rock on which she had been sitting. Her own body felt the need to stretch, but instead she pulled the shawl closer about her shoulders and gave the man a polite nod. She wanted to assure him that she would obey his order immediately.

Without another word she started down the trail that led back to the wagons. He did not walk with her, but when she had taken a few steps she heard his soft call, "G'night."

She turned then. He was still standing where she had left him. She lifted her hand, still clutching one corner of her shawl, and gave a bit of a wave. "G'night," she called back. Then she turned and ran down the trail to the waiting wagons.

Chapter Seven

Disappointment

"Captain has ridden on ahead to make some arrangements in town," said the tall man with the yellowish straggly hair. Not knowing his real name, she always thought of him as Yellow-hair. Damaris knew he was second-in-command, but she did not know another thing about him. She had always avoided him, not liking his dirty, rumpled clothing or his shifty eyes. Yellow-hair was certainly a contrast to the captain. He was tall and reed thin, while the captain was broad and stocky. Yellow-hair appeared unkempt and careless, while the captain, in spite of the long, dusty days on the trail and the intense heat, turned up each morning in a clean shirt and neatly shaven. He always found a river somewhere in which to bathe and wash his clothes.

"We should reach Poplar Crick 'long about sundown. Captain says to camp as usual. He'll meet us there on the crick bank. No one is to go into town tonight. Them's my orders. Now break camp."

He let his shifty eyes slide over the gathered throng and then wheeled his horse and left them.

Excitement filled Damaris's whole being. She shifted Edgar to her other hip and licked her dry lips. She could almost taste her freedom.

Then she suddenly realized that she was still standing dreaming while the others were busy scurrying around to break camp as they had been told. Damaris hastened to her own wagon to carry out the orders.

The girls were already there—fighting over the coveted seat again. Damaris paid them no mind and set Edgar on the ground so she could pack the last of the dishes.

It had been two days since the captain had surprised her on the bank of the small stream. She had avoided him since, thinking that he still might have some punishment in mind for her waywardness.

Damaris had her wagon loaded even before the others were ready to go. She would have gone to help Mrs. Brown, but she knew the woman had nothing much to see to. All of the camp dishes and water buckets were in the wagon that Damaris occupied. Damaris stood fidgeting, anxious to get on the trail. Surely she could endure one last day on the dusty road.

Edgar pulled at her skirt and began to whine. "Up," he cried. "Up."

Damaris bent to lift him. His arms encircled her neck and he clung closely to her.

"You know, Edgar—this is the last day I will be totin' you everywhere I go," said Damaris, sure that she would find great relief in the fact. But surprisingly, she found her own arms tightening around the small boy. A lump came into her throat and she had to swallow quickly. Edgar was a burden—but he loved her.

For the rest of the day, Damaris carried Edgar willingly. Even when she walked, trailing the wagon, she held the small boy. She did not even put him down when they finally came in sight of the town just on the other side of the small stream or when she had to begin the usual camping chores. She carried him when she went for wood. She carried him when she went to the river for water, making two trips necessary instead of the one.

It was after supper before the captain made his appearance. Damaris shrank back into the shadows of the wagon and strained to hear what he had to say to the travelers.

"Here we split," he began. "Those going to Talbert and all points south, stay on with me. Those going to Dixen and points north, stay here until Captain Trayne meets you in the mornin'. You'll git yer orders from 'im. Those stayin' on in Poplar Creek—you're home."

A cheer followed the words and the captain grinned.

"Plenty of time fer the rest of ya to git home before winter as well," the captain went on. "Tomorra is September sixteenth. Three days earlier than I had told ya I'd have ya here."

Another cheer.

But Damaris found her head spinning. It was already the fifteenth of September. She'd had no idea they had spent so many days on the trail. Along the way her fifteenth birthday had come and gone. She had no idea which day it had been in the long line of monotonous days.

The captain was speaking again.

"I need to see Willis, Rogers, and Tremount. To the rest of you—my kindest regards. May you find the West as good to you as ya expected it to be. Thank ya kindly—an' may the rest of yer trip go well."

A prolonged cheer followed those words. The captain turned to go and then turned back to the group to lift his weather-beaten hat in one last salute.

Damaris turned back to the wagon. Tomorrow they would cross to Poplar Creek.

She had sent the three girls to bed and was bending down to put away the last of the dishes when a shadow fell across her. She looked up quickly and saw the captain standing there, his worn hat held firmly in one hand.

"Miss?" he said, "may I have a moment?"

Damaris recalled the beginning of the trip when she had asked him the same question. She nodded and stood up. Edgar grabbed for her, and, without thought, she lifted the small boy into her arms.

"I went on into town today," the captain said. "Made a few inquiries. Widder woman there runs the mercantile. Says she could use some help."

Damaris didn't understand the meaning of his words. She

stood silently, looking at him with a puzzled expression in her large brown eyes.

"Says you can have the job—iffen ya'd like," the captain went on.

Damaris understood then, but her heart was too full to make any answer. She nodded again, closing her eyes briefly to hide the depths of her feelings.

"Not much fer a wage," the man went on, "but ya do git room and board, an' the room's clean an' the food good."

He seemed to be apologizing. Damaris nodded again, clutching Edgar so closely that he squirmed.

"H—how do I find her?" Damaris managed at last.

"In the mornin' just pack up yer things and walk the road thet leads to town. She's on the left—the only mercantile in the town. Ya can't miss it."

Damaris nodded again. Her mouth felt dry. She tried to swallow.

"Name is Collins. Elsa Collins—but most everyone calls her Widder Collins."

Damaris still could not speak.

"She carries 'most every necessary in her store. Even yard goods. An' she has her own machine. Maybe she'll even let ya do some of thet sewin' ya said you'd like to do."

Damaris could not believe that her dream was really about to come true.

"Well, guess thet's about it," the captain said. He placed his hat back on his head, and Damaris knew he would be leaving her.

"By the way," he said, turning after he had taken a step, "I wouldn't walk tonight. Too close to town. Seems strange—but we were safer out in the wilderness. Sometimes prowlers come in to—"

He must have seen the fear flash in her eyes.

"Oh, it's fine. Harvey and I will be on guard all night—but out there—" he nodded his head toward the darkness and did not finish the statement.

Damaris found her tongue. "I'll stay" was all she managed.

He nodded, turned, and moved away.

He was almost out of earshot before Damaris stirred herself enough to call after him, "Captain."

He turned then, the shadows almost hiding him.

"Thank you. Thank you kindly," she said, hoping she had spoken loudly enough for him to hear her.

He lifted his hat, hesitated for a moment with it in his hand, then turned again and was lost in the darkness.

Damaris had a hard time sleeping. She longed to be able to creep from the wagon and go for a walk along the stream; but she had promised the captain, and this time she would not disobey his order.

It was hard for her to believe he had taken the time to find her a job in the town. Not just a job—but a room—a real room. A clean room he said, even a machine and yard goods. Damaris fingered the dress that hung from the peg beside her. It had been worn when she left home, but now, with the fierce sun, the dusty trails, and the many washings in streams along the way, it was faded almost white and had been patched more times than she even knew.

It would be wonderful to have a new dress. One on which she would be proud to pin her mama's brooch. She closed her eyes and tried to visualize it, but her eyes popped open again. She was too restless to keep them closed.

Edgar slept soundly beside her. His soft snoring sounded like a purr to Damaris. She brushed his unruly hair from his face. Who would carry him when she was not around? Who would tell him silly little stories and sing him nursery rhymes? Who would comfort him when he cried and tell him he was a big boy when he ceased crying? Damaris was sure that his mother would be too weary and too busy to be fussing over Edgar.

Damaris pulled the little one closer and a tear escaped from beneath her long, dark lashes. Then she rebuked herself, wiped the back of her hand across her damp cheek, and willed herself to get some sleep.

———

The morning was filled with activity. Damaris hurried to light the fire and cook the morning porridge. She would have made biscuits but they were all out of flour. Mr. Brown had promised to replenish their supplies as soon as they reached a store, but there had not yet been an opportunity to enter the town.

As soon as Damaris completed her morning chores, she bundled her few belongings, checking for the hundredth time the little packet with the brooch and watch, and placed the load in readiness at the rear of the wagon.

She would need to take her leave of Mrs. Brown. She had nothing much to say to the woman, but a thank you would be in order. After all, had it not been for the family, Damaris would still be sitting back East.

Damaris hoisted Edgar onto a hip and started over to the second wagon. Mrs. Brown was just appearing from the rear opening with the crying baby in her arms.

"He still hasn't quieted none?" asked Damaris.

The woman shook her head.

"Maybe once you are settled," said Damaris, wanting to give some hope.

"Settled," said the woman wearily. "I scarce know the meanin' of the words. Seems this agony jest goes on an' on."

Damaris was puzzled by her words but made no comment.

"I came to thank you and to return Edgar," Damaris said. She wished to complete her mission and be off as quickly as possible. She had the feeling that it might be more painful than she had imagined.

"What do you mean?" the woman asked, her head lifting quickly.

"Edgar. He—he can't stay with me—now that we're here."

"But we aren't there yet."

Damaris lifted her eyes to the stream that separated them from the town. It was so near at hand and the stream was shallow. There was no reason to stay together any longer as far as she could see.

"I can walk into town," went on Damaris. "No need for me to trouble you further."

"But—you—you can't do that," said the woman.

"It's close," went on Damaris. "Why, the walk will be nothing more than a stroll. I've walked a lot farther than that—many times. And the stream is so shallow anyone could wade it."

"What are you talkin' about?" the woman asked.

Damaris saw fear or anger in her eyes, she wasn't sure which.

"We aren't stoppin' here," the woman continued.

Now it was Damaris's face that registered puzzlement and concern. What was the woman saying?

"I thought you told my husband you were goin' to settle in Dixen—like we are. He said—"

"Dixen?" repeated Damaris.

"Dixen," repeated the woman. "We set out fer Dixen—an' we ain't changed our minds none."

Damaris stood rooted to the spot.

"An' the agreement was thet you would travel with us in exchange fer a free trip."

Damaris swallowed.

"Well—am I right?" Mrs. Brown demanded.

Damaris nodded slowly. She had a job in Poplar Creek. It had sounded so right. If she went on to Dixen—wherever it was—how would she get back? She could walk—if it wasn't too far. But would the job still be waiting for her?

"Wh—where is Dixen?" Damaris asked in a choked voice.

"My husband says it's another ten or twelve days—dependin'," the woman answered. Then she brushed the hair from her face with a tired hand. "Don't know how I'll ever be standin' it," she spoke sadly.

Damaris turned and walked away. She was afraid that tears were going to start to flow. She had never felt such disappointment in her entire life. She had to find some way to let Widow Collins know she couldn't accept the job. Ten to twelve days! Ten or twelve more days on the trail. She didn't know how she'd ever stand it either.

Chapter Eight

In Camp

Damaris awoke the next morning to a drizzling rain. As she listened to the patter on the canvas overhead, she wished she could turn over and go back to sleep. Edgar stirred and reached for her but Damaris drew back. Yesterday she had prepared herself to say farewell to Edgar. Knowing it would bring pain, she had steeled herself against it. Now she would need to repeat the procedure, and she didn't know how her fragile emotions could endure any more. For the next ten or twelve days she would hold Edgar at a distance. He would not take possession of her devotion again.

The fire needs to be built, she told herself as she snuggled beneath the blanket to gain as much warmth as possible before facing the coldness of the day. Damaris was thankful she had gathered extra wood and tucked it under the wagon where it would be dry.

At last she crawled reluctantly from her bed and managed, in the tightness of the small wagon, to squirm out of her simple sleeping garment and into her much-mended petticoat and colorless dress.

The morning was even colder than she expected. She wished she could bundle her shawl about her shoulders, but shawls were dangerous around morning fires. Back on the trail a woman had been badly burned when her shawl had dangled into the flames and caught on fire. Had not a man been passing by who quickly rolled her on the ground to put out the fire, her injuries might have been even worse. So Damaris left her shawl behind and shivered as she started the fire with trembling, cold fingers.

At the other side of the camp there was already a lot of commotion and Damaris remembered, with an aching heart, that the wagon master and nine wagons from the train would soon be off toward the south.

It reminded her again of the job that awaited her in town.

"I could just run off," she murmured to herself. "I could hide until the Browns have left—and then go into Poplar Creek and take that job the captain found for me."

But even as she whispered her thoughts, Damaris knew she could never do such a thing. She had made a promise. She owed the Browns for her passage west.

The fire was going and the coffee boiling when Mr. Brown appeared. He looked about as cold as Damaris felt and she could see by the wetness of his woollen shirt that he had been up for some time. He looked miserable, and Damaris concluded that he had been out in the rain caring for the horses and other chores about camp.

"My missus is gonna lay abed," he said to Damaris, pouring himself a mug of coffee from the pot. "Baby kept her awake fer most of the night."

Damaris nodded.

"I'm goin' on into town fer supplies. We expect the new wagon master about noon an' we need to be ready to roll soon as he gives the order."

Damaris didn't even nod. She knew what duties needed to be done before they would be ready to roll.

"Anything you needin' from town?"

His question surprised Damaris. She hadn't expected him to think of her. She shook her head slowly, admitting to herself that she needed just about everything.

Then she raised her eyes slowly, drawing a quick breath so she wouldn't lose her courage. "Are you going to the mercantile?" she asked.

He nodded, looking at her over the cup of coffee.

"Would you—could you give the lady there a message for me?"

Damaris would have preferred to have written the woman a note, but she had no pen or paper.

Mr. Brown nodded again.

"The—the captain—he talked to her—about me getting a job in her store. Could you tell her that I—I won't be staying on in Poplar Creek but—I—I sure do 'preciate the offer."

Mr. Brown's eyes opened wide as she made her little speech. Apparently Mrs. Brown had said nothing to him about their previous conversation.

Damaris allowed her eyes to turn back to the fire. "I—I didn't know you weren't stopping here," she added quietly as an explanation.

Mr. Brown shifted on his log seat. Damaris continued stirring the morning porridge without looking up.

"I think thet's good enough," he said to her. "I'm in rather a hurry."

Damaris dished the porridge and handed him his plate. She felt her own stomach heave. It was bad enough trying to down the gruel, unsavory as it was without milk or sugar, but to eat it half-raw, that was even worse.

But Mr. Brown went right to work, washing down the unappetizing food with long gulps of weak coffee.

He stood and cast a glance at the sky. There was no break in the cloudy curtain that closed them in.

"Get the kids up," he said to Damaris. "I need to take thet wagon to town fer supplies. I was gonna drive the other wagon but I don't want to bother Mrs. Brown."

Damaris moved to obey but her thoughts were heavy. With their wagon gone and Mrs. Brown sleeping in the other, how would she ever get through the morning with four youngsters out in the rain?

Mr. Brown did not notice her concern. He had thought of another item to add to his long list and had reached into his pocket to draw it out. As he unfolded his little bit of paper, Damaris saw the bills tucked inside it.

She drew in her breath with a quick gulp of air. *He has*

money! And he's heading to town! Damaris knew what that meant. They likely wouldn't see him for the rest of the day and when he did appear again—there would be trouble—for all of them.

With a quick step she went to awaken the children. She did not want Mr. Brown to be annoyed when he left. That might make him even more irritable and mean when he returned after a day at the saloon.

The three girls were not happy about the new day. They fussed and quarreled and lagged as Damaris tried to hurry them. Edgar awoke without too much grumbling but wanted to cling to Damaris for warmth and comfort, while all she wanted was to get him dressed and out of the wagon. When they all finally emerged no one was in a good mood.

"It's cold out here," moaned Nina, and Trudy echoed the words.

"Why do we have to come out in the rain?" cried Bella.

"Your pa is going to town," answered Damaris.

"Why can't we go?" asked Trudy.

"He doesn't wish to take you," answered Damaris, almost as sour as the others.

"I'm cold."

"Wrap your shawl closer," advised Damaris.

"It doesn't help. It's still cold."

"Yes," said Damaris, "it is cold—and it is going to get much colder, so no use fussing about it."

Damaris decided to try to keep the fire going. At least there would be some comfort from the heat.

Conrad was just finishing his breakfast when Damaris and the children reached the shelter where the breakfast fire flamed. He didn't even nod at Damaris or speak to his sisters as he spooned in the last few mouthfuls.

"Bet yer goin' with Pa," accused Bella.

Conrad nodded his head but did not look up.

"It's not fair!" cried Nina.

He did look up then. Damaris thought she could read anger or resignation in his eyes.

"You wanna carry heavy sacks and crates to load the

wagon?" His voice was low and controlled—but also weary—and Damaris suddenly realized that he was a very young boy to have been doing a man's job for the many, many miles of crossing the prairies.

She stole a look at him and noticed how the coarse shirt hung loosely over his thin shoulders. She was sure he had lost weight, and he had not been big for his age at the beginning of the trip.

"Where's Pa?" pouted Nina.

"Gittin' the horses," Conrad replied. Then he put down his empty plate and turned to go.

"It's not fair," Trudy flung after him, but he did not turn around or indicate in any way that he had heard her.

Damaris began to dish up plates of the morning porridge.

"I hate this stuff," said Nina. "It tastes like—like slop."

"How do you know what slop tastes like?" asked Bella. "Did you ever eat it?"

"I smelled it," declared Nina hotly.

Trudy began to giggle. "Nina's eating slo-op. Nina's eatin' slo-op," she said in a sing-songy voice.

Nina reached over and slapped her and the fight began. Damaris knew they were in for a very long day.

———————

"I hear there's been a change of plans?"

The voice behind Damaris brought her quickly to an upright position. She had been bending over the porridge pot, scrubbing it with a handful of creek-bed sand. The wagon master stood there, his hat droopy with the morning rain, his shoulders seeming to sag under the weight of his wet shirt.

Her dark eyes clouded and she nodded slowly in verification.

"I'm sorry," he said softly.

Damaris swallowed hard and tried to straighten her slight shoulders. "I did have an agreement," she answered in a barely audible voice.

"Perhaps you'll find an even better job in Dixen," the

wagon master tried to console her.

Damaris reached down to brush sand from the skirt of her dress.

"I've brought you a—a letter of reference," he went on as he reached into his shirt pocket and withdrew a folded piece of paper. "I don't know iffen you'll even need this—but I thought it could do no harm."

Damaris was surprised at his consideration. He had been so kind to her—he who had not wanted her on his wagon train in the first place.

"I—I thank you," she fumbled as she accepted the bit of paper. "I—I most 'preciate it."

They stood in silence for a moment. She let her eyes study the toes of her worn shoes. She felt him move beside her.

"Well—I must be going. We're 'bout ready to push on."

Damaris looked up then. His broad shoulders had straightened and he lifted the hat from his head and shook the water from the dripping brim. She was surprised at the amount of gray in his hair.

"I do hope," he said sincerely, "thet all goes well fer you. Brown says he won't leave you stranded. Will try to get ya located in town before he moves on to his homestead."

Damaris was surprised at the statement. The captain must have had a chat with Mr. Brown.

"Thank ya," she said in a whispery voice and lowered her eyes again.

He reached out his hand to her. Damaris couldn't remember shaking hands with a man before and she felt embarrassed. She brushed her soiled hands quickly on her skirts before she extended her hand to meet his.

"God bless ya, miss," said the man, looking directly into her eyes.

Damaris had never heard such concern and sincerity in a man's voice. She could not speak, so she just nodded and swallowed hard. Then the captain withdrew his hand, turned, and was gone.

It was several moments before Damaris knelt again in the sand and continued cleaning the pot.

As she worked, still pondering the captain's parting words, she heard the familiar sounds of wagons moving out from camp. She turned to watch the smaller train wend its way through the morning mist.

Sadness filled her heart, though she couldn't understand why. She scarcely knew the captain. In fact, she was still afraid of him in some ways—but he had spoken kindly to her. Had even taken the time to find her a job—to write a letter of recommendation. And he had asked nothing in return. That was what puzzled Damaris. And she had never seen him drunk. Not once in the many days on the trail. Oh, true, there were no saloons along the way. But even when he had gone into town, he returned sober. She had not smelled liquor on his breath the few times he had stood close enough that she would have been able to detect it. Was it possible that not all men were like her pa?

———————

It was almost noon before Damaris sighted the returning Brown wagon. The girls must have spotted it about the same time, for Damaris heard a clamor from the shelter by the fire.

"It's Pa!" one screeched, and the others soon joined her.

Damaris shifted the sleeping Edgar in her arms. The yelling would waken him for sure. She rocked him gently and pulled the blanket up more closely around his ears.

Now we are in for it—all of us, thought Damaris. *I hate the thought of it.*

But the girls were dancing under the tree-strung tarp and continuing to yell. "Pa's comin'. Pa's comin'." There didn't seem to be any worry or concern in any of their faces.

And sure enough, when the wagon arrived and Mr. Brown "whoa'd" the team and climbed down from the wagon, he seemed as sober as when he had driven off to town.

"Did ya bring us anything?"

"Did ya get sweets?"

"Did ya, Pa?"

The noise got louder and Mr. Brown laughed and rumpled

wet hair with a large calloused hand. Finally he pulled a small bag from his pocket and passed it to Bella with instructions to share equally. "An' don't fergit Damaris," he added.

Damaris looked up in surprise. She still had not gotten over the shock of a sober employer—and then to be offered a sweet besides. Damaris could not believe her ears and eyes.

"We'll need to hurry," he said almost apologetically. "We saw the train in the distance, movin' this way."

Damaris nodded and moved toward the wagon to lay Edgar in the bed. When she lifted the flap, she could scarcely believe her eyes. There were no beds. New supplies were stacked everywhere.

"We'll have to sort thet all out this evenin'," Mr. Brown said. "We can put a good share of it in the other wagon when we stop fer the night. Right now we need to eat so we're ready to travel. I had them put things fer today's meals in thet there box nearest ya."

Damaris looked down at the sleeping Edgar. There was no place to lay him. She would have to rouse him and get on with the task of preparing the meal.

"Give 'im to me," said Mr. Brown. "I'll take 'im on over to the Missus."

Damaris handed over the small boy, feeling much relieved. He was always so fussy when awakened early from a nap, and she knew he would have hung on her skirts and insisted on being held while she tried desperately to build the fire and get the meal cooked as quickly as possible.

As Mr. Brown moved off to the other wagon with the sleeping boy, Damaris headed for the wagon to get supplies and start their dinner.

Mr. Brown hadn't taken many steps before he turned and called back, "By the way, the woman was right sorry thet you weren't comin' in to work. Captain must have given her quite a report."

Chapter Nine

Traveling On

For eleven more days they rattled on in the wagons. Damaris walked as frequently as her tired feet and worn shoes allowed her some degree of comfort. If the track was even, she kicked off the shoes and walked barefooted. The soles of her feet were so calloused that it took sharp rocks or briars to penetrate them.

The girls fussed, Edgar clung, and Mrs. Brown continued to keep to her wagon, appearing only at mealtime. She looked haggard and pale, and the baby still cried and could not be comforted.

Damaris wondered if he was getting enough to eat, but never having had anything to do with babies, she dared not ask.

On the eleventh day they topped a ridge, and there beneath them lay the little town of Dixen. It didn't look like much. A few scattered, crude buildings huddled together on the edge of a clump of straggly pines. Open prairie stretched out toward the north and east, and broken foothills with patches of timber reached to the west and swung around to the south. Damaris was disappointed. She had liked the look of Poplar Creek much better.

At the same time, she felt relief. It would be so good to arrive. To finally be where they were going. To get in out of the sun and wind. To sleep at night with room to properly turn over. To put down her burdens of water buckets, firewood—and Edgar. But she did hope there was more to this little town than showed at first appearance.

She reached for her apron pocket to feel the safety pin that held the small packet containing watch, brooch, and letter of reference firmly in place. It always gave her a measure of security to note that it was still there.

The wagons finally bumped to a stop, and Captain Trayne called an assembly. As soon as folks had tethered their teams and gathered around, Captain Trayne spoke.

"We have reached our destination. I will leave you here. You can make your own way into the town, each going his separate way from there.

"There is an office on the main street thet deals with land claims and serves as the local bank. Iffen ya have any doubt as to where to find yer land—stop there fer directions."

Without any further farewell or any words of best wishes, the captain wheeled his horse and was off. Damaris thought he must be as tired of the whole procedure as she herself.

She turned back to the wagon and noticed that Mrs. Brown had emerged, patting and rocking the wailing baby as she moved forward.

"I s'pose you'll be leavin' us now," she offered, and Damaris nodded.

They stood a few feet apart, Edgar clinging to Damaris, the baby crying in his mother's arms.

"I don't know what I woulda done without ya," Mrs. Brown admitted.

Looking at her pale, strained face, Damaris felt a pang of pity.

"Will you be all right, ma'am?" Damaris asked before she could check herself.

"I'll manage," said the woman, but she did not smile and she did not seem too confident. "My husband says it's only a few hours further."

"Are you—are you goin' right on?"

"As soon as he takes you into town. The captain made him promise."

Damaris nodded. She had heard of that promise, but she

wished she could wave it aside. She was sure she would fare much better on her own than Mrs. Brown would with the children.

"I—I'll be fine—" she started, but the woman interrupted.

"A promise is a promise!"

Damaris nodded her head. *A promise is a promise* echoed in her mind.

Mr. Brown appeared just as Damaris turned to go.

"Are you ready?" he asked, and Damaris looked at the child still in her arms.

"Leave him here with his ma," Mr. Brown said, his voice sounding impatient.

Damaris leaned over to place the boy on the ground, but Edgar clung to her neck. He had no intention of being deserted. When Damaris unwrapped the twining fingers, he screamed and clutched at her skirts. Damaris tried gently to loosen his grip, but he clung the harder, his wailing becoming louder and more persistent.

Mrs. Brown was helpless. She already had one crying baby in her arms.

"Where's Trudy?" grumbled Mr. Brown. Then he shouted her name. "Trudy! Trudy, your ma needs some help here."

While he called and paced, Damaris kept trying to free herself from the screaming Edgar.

At length Trudy appeared, Nina and Bella trailing along behind her.

"Help yer ma," said Mr. Brown. "Look after yer brother."

At length Damaris was able to pass Edgar to Trudy, but he went reluctantly, crying and kicking and screaming for "Da'mis."

Damaris walked away, her back stiff and her head up, but her lip trembling.

Every fiber of her being wanted to turn and run back to the young child. She wanted to cling to him just as tightly as he wished to cling to her. She wanted to hoist him to her hip and carry him on into town. She wanted to whisper to him that he would never have to leave her—but Damaris was not free to do as she wanted.

Even from the wagon where Damaris went to retrieve her belongings, she could hear wails of "Da'mis, Da'mis," and Damaris knew the boy would continue to ask for her long after she was gone.

Her heart ached as she gathered her little bundle and stumbled along the rutted trail beside the man who intended to keep his promise.

The town did not look any more promising close up than it had from a distance. The building the wagon master had spoken of as the bank and title office was the sturdiest building in town. It even had some paint on its facade. The only other building to make that boast was a building at the far end of the street that proclaimed "Saloon." Damaris shivered as she looked at it.

Between the two buildings Damaris identified a large store with dingy windows, a tiny shop that doubled as a dwelling, displaying a neat sign saying, "Miss Dover—Seamstress," and a building with a handwritten notice in the window that said, "Miners Supplies." Across the street signs advertised a livery, a boardinghouse, a blacksmith, and another store that seemed to be the competition. There were other scattered buildings, but Damaris was not able to identify their use. Setting apart on this side or that were crude houses, most of them not much more than cabins. The simple farm home Damaris had left was better than the majority.

Mr. Brown suddenly realized that she had been carrying a bundle and reached down to take it from her just as they reached the board sidewalk that fronted the saloon. Damaris was tempted to resist his offer, but somewhat reluctantly yielded her possessions. She didn't have much—but it felt good to be able to cling to something.

Damaris couldn't see much beyond the saloon and she wondered just where they were going when Mr. Brown made a sharp turn and indicated the saloon door.

She hesitated, stopping and looking at him with questioning eyes.

"Go in," he urged her, giving his hand a little wave to usher her forward.

"It's a—a saloon," she choked, taking a small step backward.

"Thet's where we are to find Gordon."

"Who's Gordon?"

"I was told to find 'im here," he said as though that was explanation enough.

"B—but I don't wish to—to make the acquaintance of a—a saloon keeper," insisted Damaris, and she stubbornly backed up another step.

"The captain said to bring you here," the man went on, impatience now edging his voice.

"But—I—I don't wish to work in a saloon," maintained Damaris, her chin lifting.

The man was really impatient now. "Look," he said pointedly. "I have a wife and family back there waitin' fer me to git them on out to our land. I don't expect thet they are havin' an easy time waitin'. Now—I made a promise—an' I plan to keep it. The captain said, 'See Gordon at the saloon.' Now let's git on with it and see Gordon."

Damaris's back stiffened. She had no intention of working in a saloon, even if she had to starve to death. She felt disappointed and angry with the captain. Surely he knew better than to send her to a saloon for a job.

Mr. Brown took her arm, urging her forward, and Damaris took a deep breath and stepped through the door. She would never be rid of the man if she didn't cooperate, she reasoned, but as soon as he was gone, she would vacate the offensive place and look for work on her own.

"Can I help you?" someone asked.

Damaris's eyes had not adjusted to the dimness of the lighting, so she could not see who spoke.

"We're lookin' fer Gordon," said Mr. Brown.

"He's across the street at the jailhouse," said the voice. "First building down to the left."

"Oh, my," Damaris moaned under her breath. "First a saloon and now the jail."

She turned on her heel and left the place even before Mr. Brown had gathered his wits. What a relief to be back in the open air, the smell of whiskey and cigars left behind her.

Mr. Brown surveyed the street and picked out the building mentioned. "Right over there," he said to her, steering
her forward with his voice.

Damaris said nothing. When it came down to it, she preferred the jail to the saloon.

They climbed the wooden steps and stopped at the open
door. Two men sat at a small table. They held cards, and
Damaris knew she and Mr. Brown were interrupting their
game. In front of them sat a bottle of whiskey and two half-
empty glasses. At the sound of the footsteps, both men looked
up. One was chewing the end of a cigar butt, the other, the
one with the trimmed mustache, had a wad of chewing tobacco tucked in his cheek. Damaris knew immediately that
she did not wish to work for either of them.

"Help ya?" asked the one with the cigar, shifting it with
his tongue as he spoke.

"Lookin' fer Gordon," said Mr. Brown.

"Thet's me," said the man, his eyes narrowing to a squint.

"Captain Reilly said to look ya up. Miss—Miss Damaris
here aims to stay on in town. Needs work an' a place to live."

Damaris felt herself being appraised by two pairs of prob-
ing eyes. She knew the color was rising in her cheeks.

The tobacco chewer spit on the board floor and his mustache twitched.

The man named Gordon leaned forward slowly, laid aside
his cards with deliberate motion, and pushed back from the
table.

"Need work, huh?" he asked, his eyes on Damaris.

Damaris could not speak. It was all she could do to give
a slight nod.

"What kinda work ya do?" asked the man.

"I—I—" stammered Damaris, unable to answer.

Mr. Brown cut in. "She's right good with kids. Can cook
fair-to-middlin', ain't afraid of household chores or totin'
wood an' water," he said.

Gordon nodded.

"Understand she has a letter of recommend from the captain," went on Mr. Brown. Damaris reached into her pocket to safeguard her precious letter. She had no intention of releasing it to Mr. Gordon.

Mr. Gordon shifted his cigar again, his eyes still on Damaris.

"Might do," he said at length, and he finished the last of the whiskey in his glass, reached for his hat, and stood up.

"B—but I don't—don't wish to work for you," Damaris stuttered, finding courage in spite of her trembling body.

"Fer me?" The man halted mid-stride and looked at Damaris, his eyes wide with wonder. "Fer me? What ya think I would want with a girl like you?"

The man still at the table broke forth in a loud guffaw, slapping his knee and rocking in his chair until Gordon wheeled and gave him a dark look.

"Captain never woulda sent ya to work fer me, girlie," said Gordon, settling his dusty hat on his head. "He jest knows I know everything thet goes on in this here little hick town. No sirree. Captain never woulda sent ya to work fer me."

Damaris felt a wave of relief wash over her body.

"C'mon," the man said, with a nod toward the door, "let's git ya outer here and over to Mrs. Stacy. She might figger out something."

There seemed nothing for Damaris to do but follow.

They clumped along the wooden sidewalk and turned in at the gate that led to the boardinghouse. Gordon did not stop to knock on the door but walked right on into a wide entry and hollered to announce his arrival. "Hallo. Anyone here?"

Damaris could hear stirring in a room beyond. It wasn't long until a woman appeared. She was dressed simply, her graying hair gathered and placed in a loose knot at the top of her head. Her lips were tightly pressed and her nose a bit long, but Damaris thought she detected warmth in the woman's eyes.

"Brought this here girlie in to see iffen ya might need

some help," said Gordon with no attempt at introductions or small talk.

Damaris felt the intense eyes survey her thoroughly.

"She has a letter of recommend," cut in Mr. Brown. He nudged Damaris out of her stupor. "Show 'er."

Damaris fumbled with the pin and eventually was able to produce the letter. The woman read it in silence as Damaris held her breath. At last she looked up and Damaris thought she heard a sigh.

"I can give you work, right enough," she said. Her voice was soft and almost motherly, and Damaris felt her heart racing. "But I can't give you much for pay."

"Even board and room," cut in Mr. Brown.

Damaris looked down at her badly worn clothing. Board and room wouldn't be quite enough.

"Hear Miss Dover needs some help—maybe between the two of us—" She did not finish her sentence. She looked at Damaris again.

"Well—we'll see if we can work out something. Mr. MacKenzie might even need a hand now an' then with the store."

"You'll keep her, then?" asked Mr. Brown in a way that reminded Damaris of how anxious he was to have his obligation fulfilled.

Mrs. Stacy nodded. "Come in," she said to Damaris; then to Mr. Brown she added, "Bring her things in."

Mr. Brown held up the small bundle. "Got 'em all right here," he hastened to inform her.

Damaris didn't miss the look of shocked surprise that flashed through the woman's eyes.

"Well, bring it right into this small bedroom off the kitchen," she said, leading the way.

Damaris stood rooted to the spot. She wasn't sure if she should follow or stay where she was. The man Gordon shifted his weight restlessly, as though he too was anxious to have his duty over.

"Thank you for your help, sir," said Damaris with a slight nod.

He turned and left then, as unceremoniously as he had entered.

Mr. Brown was the next to go. He seemed very anxious and hardly stopped long enough to shake hands with Damaris and Mrs. Stacy.

As soon as the door closed behind him, Damaris sucked in her breath. She had never felt any particular attachment to Mr. Brown, but with his going all ties with anything known were severed. It was a frightening feeling and she shivered involuntarily.

"Would you like a warm bath, my dear?" Mrs. Stacy was asking. "There's plenty of time fer you to take one before we need to prepare the evening meal."

Damaris looked down at her dusty, mended clothing and realized just how she must look in the eyes of the tidy woman before her. She nodded her head dumbly, at the same time her mind scrambled to think of what she could put on after her bath. But Mrs. Stacy was speaking again.

"I have plenty of aprons. They will almost wrap 'round you twice . . ." She hesitated, seeming to rethink what she was about to say. "At least they'll keep the dinner off your dress."

Damaris took another deep breath. With the trail dust washed from her body and hair and her mended dress covered by the ample apron, perhaps she would be able to present some kind of acceptable appearance.

Chapter Ten

A New Life Begins

As soon as Damaris had bathed and her dark hair was partially dried, she put on her one clean dress and reported to the kitchen. The room was filled with the smell of cooking dinner and the clatter of pots.

Mrs. Stacy was there, bending over the oven, sticking a plump roasting hen with the tine of a fork.

"It'll be done," she said without lifting her head, her voice sounding relieved that the bird in question would be ready for the meal ahead.

"Where would you like me to start?" asked Damaris hesitantly.

"I need two buckets of water from the well out back," said Mrs. Stacy as she straightened and looked at Damaris. Damaris could feel the warm eyes travel from her face to her dress and back again.

"The aprons are on a peg in the pantry," she added.

Damaris moved forward to find one.

As the lady had said, the apron was almost big enough to wrap around Damaris twice. She felt relief as she folded it about her and tied the strings at her waist. Then she picked up the two buckets and went in search of the well.

It was not hard to find. Behind the boardinghouse stood an enclosed yard. The well was located in the middle with a pen for fowl at the one side and an ample garden on the other. Damaris noted that Mrs. Stacy must grow a good deal of what she served. Excitement filled her. It would be almost like being back on the farm.

She did not dally with the water buckets and was soon depositing them on the long, low counter from which she had taken them.

"Put some in that big kettle," Mrs. Stacy instructed, and Damaris moved to do so.

From then on the two worked together, Damaris often anticipating her employer's wishes before she spoke them.

Damaris soon learned that Mrs. Stacy served meals as well as kept boarders. There was no accommodation or restaurant in the town except at Mrs. Stacy's. Anyone wishing a place to board, a bed for the night when passing through, or a meal before returning to some distant residence stopped there.

The trick in running the small accommodation was not just being ready to serve, but guessing how many might need the service.

Damaris was eager to learn and quick to catch on. By the time the first two guests had arrived, the table was set and the smell of supper was penetrating the small dining area.

Damaris watched carefully as Mrs. Stacy moved hurriedly about the rooms—from kitchen to dining table, back to kitchen. Damaris had never served tables before, but she judged it to be within her capability.

In all, they served seven guests—Mr. Gordon, whom she learned was Sheriff Gordon, and his mustached friend being two of them. A farmer from some distance stopped in for a meal and bed. He was in town for supplies and would leave for home early in the morning, he said. Three rough-looking young men came in together, and Damaris felt their eyes on her as she moved about the room. She was glad for the sheriff's presence.

The three men moved on without incident, and Damaris hurried to clear the empty table and take the dirty dishes to the kitchen. The sheriff and his friend also left the dining room. Then a man came in alone, and Mrs. Stacy seemed pleased to see him. "I'll look after Mr. Hebert," she said, and

Damaris went back to clearing tables. She noticed that Mrs. Stacy called the man "Sam" when she spoke with him.

Damaris had the dishes washed and placed back in the cupboards by the time Mrs. Stacy came in from the dining room carrying the dishes used by the man named Sam.

"Sam needs a room," she said to Damaris. "Would you check on the little one at the head of the stairs. Pull the shade, light the lamp, and turn back the blankets."

Damaris wiped her hands on her apron and moved quickly to do as bidden.

When she returned to the kitchen, she could still hear voices in the dining room. Damaris finished her task and stood idly. She was so tired she could hardly stand. She wondered what duties might still be expected of her before retiring, but she hated to interrupt the conversation in the next room.

At last Damaris left the kitchen with the two heavy buckets. At least she could fill them for morning. She placed the buckets back on the stand and turned to the woodbox. She had no idea where the wood was kept, so she went to investigate. She soon found the small shed housing the wood supply and filled the box until it was heaped. Then she went back to the yard to check on the hens and fasten the door to the coop.

Damaris returned to the kitchen, still unsure as to what she should do next. She swept the floor and wiped off the stove, but still the voices droned on in the next room.

Damaris paced to the window and lifted the curtain. Night was falling. The town was dark and deserted. All she could see was the faint glow of lamplight from windows along the street.

Damaris heard some rowdy laughter and saw the three young men leave the saloon and boisterously mount their horses. They left with raucous shouts and a cloud of dust.

Damaris tapped her foot impatiently, wishing that she might either be assigned a task or allowed to retire.

Finally Mrs. Stacy entered the kitchen, two cups held in her hands.

"Oh, my dear," she said when she saw Damaris, "I had quite forgotten about you. You must be dreadfully tired. Go on to bed now. I'll see to—" Then she stopped and looked about the tidy kitchen. "Oh my," she said, "it looks like you have already finished everything there was to do. Run on, now. Get some rest."

Damaris was only too glad to accept her invitation.

As she climbed between the fresh sheets, she realized that it was the first time in many weeks she'd had a bed all to herself. Calmness settled about her. She had arrived, and she had a job. She had a nice, simple room all to herself and a pleasant woman to work for.

She thought again of the captain and realized that much of this was his doing. She wondered where he was, wishing she could write to him to express her thankfulness.

Damaris stretched her feet into the blankets and shifted her body to the most comfortable position. Things had really gone quite well for her. But as she lay in the comfortable bed trying to enjoy her pleasant circumstance, she felt an unexplainable emptiness within. She could not understand it until she put her arm out in the darkness and realized that without thinking she had reached for Edgar. Damaris knew the feeling then. She ached for the young boy. She wondered if he was still crying for her. Damaris would not allow tears to flow, but her heart ached with the intensity of her loneliness.

———

"We will go and meet Miss Dover," said Mrs. Stacy as soon as the breakfast had been served and the dishes washed and put away.

Damaris nodded. She was quite happy with her circumstance and was tempted to say that she would be willing to work for room and board, after all. The big aprons hid her dress nicely. But then her eyes fell to her shoes and she realized that she would soon be needing a new pair. Fall was approaching and the shoes she was wearing would never get her through the winter.

She nodded reluctantly and removed her apron just as Mrs. Stacy had done. How she wished she could have left it on.

The two crossed the street and walked along the boardwalk to the little building with Miss Dover's sign out front. Mrs. Stacy stopped long enough to dingle the bell at the door and then walked right on in.

They were greeted by a woman with strange spectacles resting on the tip of her nose. She was plump and smiling and looked pleased with the world in which she lived.

"Mrs. Stacy," she said with a lilt to her voice, "how nice to see you."

Mrs. Stacy returned the greeting, then turned to Damaris. "This is Damaris Withers. She is new in town. Just got in yesterday. Came in with a train. Had a most impressive letter of reference—and, I might add, has more than lived up to it already. She's working fer me—but I really don't need her full time. Can't really afford to pay her as much as she is worth. You said once thet there are times when you could use some help here. Is that still so?"

Damaris felt the soft gray eyes turn to her. A full smile was on the woman's lips. Miss Dover reached out a hand and placed it gently on Damaris's arm.

"Welcome to Dixen, my dear," she said warmly.

Damaris liked her at once.

"Do you sew?" Miss Dover asked first.

Damaris wished she could honestly have stated that she was very good with a needle and thread—or with one of the machines used for sewing—but she could not. She shook her head slowly, concern showing in her face. "I've only mended, ma'am," she admitted.

"Well, no bother," said the woman with a pat on the arm she had touched. "I expect that you'll catch on quickly enough when given the chance." Then she brightened further. "Besides, mending is more than half of my business. I could sure use someone who knows how to mend."

"Then it is decided?" asked Mrs. Stacy.

Miss Dover nodded. "Send her over whenever you run out

of work," she said. "I'll see if I can keep her busy."

"I was going to try Mr. MacKenzie as well," went on Mrs. Stacy.

Miss Dover thought about it for a few moments. "That would be wise," she said at last. "Between the three of us, we should be able to fill her days with duties."

Damaris wished she didn't have to extend herself all over town, but she was thankful to be working at all.

"Can you stop for tea?" asked Miss Dover.

"I would love to, but our time is limited and we must hurry if we are to see Mr. MacKenzie."

The ladies bid each other a good-day, and Mrs. Stacy and Damaris moved on.

It was only a short distance to the large square building that sat at the end of the main street. Two wagons were tied in front of it, and a saddle horse stomped and blew at a nearby post. Damaris could not take her eyes off the lone horse. He reminded her of the horse her pa had back home.

They passed into the dimly lit building. Damaris stood for a few moments allowing her eyes to get used to the darkness. The storekeeper was busy with customers, so Mrs. Stacy passed by the counter and over to the yard goods. She fingered several pieces of material and Damaris thought she saw longing in her eyes.

"My, this is a lovely piece," she said of a dark brocade. Then her hand moved on to another, "And look at this calico. Isn't it soft and feminine?"

Damaris had to admit that it was. She was surprised at the good stock of yard goods at such a small, out-of-the-way town.

"People drive in for miles to shop here," said Mrs. Stacy as though reading Damaris's mind. "No other town for miles."

Damaris wished she felt the freedom to let the soft materials slip through her hands, but she remembered her mama scolding and telling her that children were not to touch the store stock.

Damaris moved away from the shelves, more to resist

temptation than because she was curious about the rest of the store. She had taken only a few steps when she noticed the shoes. There weren't many styles to choose from, but Damaris spotted a pair that she would love to own. They looked so soft, so comfortable, and yet so stylish. Damaris pictured them on her own slender feet. But when she looked at the price, her breath caught in her throat. She would never have that much money.

Mrs. Stacy moved forward as soon as the last customer left.

"Mr. MacKenzie," she began even before she had reached the counter where the man waited. "I'd like you to meet Miss Withers. She has just joined us. Came in on yesterday's train. She is working part time for me and part time for Miss Dover, but she still has some available hours if you'd like some help now and then here in your store. She has a letter of reference—and I must say it paints a glowing picture of her ambitiousness—which I have found, in one brief day, to be quite true."

She stopped for a breath, and Mr. MacKenzie looked at Damaris.

"Been to school?" he asked bluntly.

Damaris nodded.

"You'll need to know yer sums if ya plan to work here."

Damaris nodded again. She had never had trouble with sums.

"'Course you could do sweeping and stockin' shelves and such. Mrs. MacKenzie never seems to find much time for it anymore."

"About how many days would you need her?" said Mrs. Stacy.

"Two. Part time. Two—part time—should do. I'll let you know when I figure it more closely."

They left for home then, Mrs. Stacy feeling quite good about their outing.

"Well," she said with satisfaction. "Looks like it will work out just fine. Mr. MacKenzie will take you a couple days—part time—an' he'll put your wage on account. You ought to

92

be able to buy some shoes come winter an' maybe even a piece of yard goods. And Miss Dover will take you a couple days—part time. You'll sew for her in exchange for a wage. An' you'll have your board an' room with me in exchange for your help there. That should work out just fine."

Damaris supposed it would. She knew she should be truly thankful, but she couldn't shake the feeling that she had just been pieced out here and there. She wondered if she would ever have anything at all to say about her own life.

Chapter Eleven

Miss Dover

Damaris hadn't thought much about Christmas until she heard Mrs. Stacy make references to "celebrating" it. The idea frightened Damaris, though she didn't dare say so. In her mind were vivid memories of how her father had "celebrated" any event that gave him an excuse to drink.

On Christmas Day Damaris worked hard, hoping that if she finished all her chores she would be free to escape to the safety of her own room.

But Mrs. Stacy did not let her go so easily. "Slip into your prettiest dress, Damaris," she suggested. "Folks will soon be here for our little Christmas celebration."

Damaris grew weak and pale. She placed a trembling hand on the table for support. Mrs. Stacy noticed, and she watched Damaris a moment with concern on her face.

"What is it?" she asked. "Don't you feel well?"

"I—I don't think so," mumbled Damaris.

Mrs. Stacy placed a hand on the girl's forehead.

"You don't seem to have a fever."

"I—I just feel—" began Damaris.

"Perhaps you should go lie down. I can manage things. If you feel better you may join us later."

Damaris crept off, relieved to be released from attending the celebration.

Later she heard voices and laughter and even some singing, but she stayed curled in a ball, huddled under her blankets. Her ears were attuned to hear glass breaking, the banging of chairs being overturned, or shouts of anger, but those sounds never came.

And then everything was quiet. Mrs. Stacy came to her room and knocked gently on the door.

"Are you sleeping?" she whispered, opening the door a crack. "Can I get you anything? A drink? Water or cold buttermilk?"

Damaris would have given anything for a glass of cold water, but she licked her dry lips and shook her head.

"I'll be fine," she managed.

Mrs. Stacy bid her a Merry Christmas and closed her door.

It seemed to Damaris that she was always on the run. She would just be settled into a task at Mrs. Stacy's when word would come that she was needed at Mr. MacKenzie's store. Or she would be hanging up the broom at the store and Mr. MacKenzie would say, "You can hustle over to Miss Dover's now. I won't need you anymore today."

She tried to convince herself that she really didn't mind. That it kept her from boredom. That it acquainted her with the people of the town. That she was young and the exercise did her good. But in spite of all the reasoning she did with herself, Damaris longed for a sense of actually belonging— somewhere.

The little jobs here and there, which often turned into big jobs before the day was over, were slowly paying for the new shoes on her feet and the two new dresses in her closet. Damaris had found it hard to wear her precious dresses for her working duties, so Miss Dover had altered, free of charge, two of her own old ones for Damaris to wear for daily tasks.

Damaris was thankful. She admired her two new dresses and wouldn't want to soil them—but with working seven days a week, she really had little occasion to wear them.

Her days often stretched from early breakfast preparation to late-night dishes, with many, many errands and tasks in between. Every night Damaris fell into bed so weary that she seldom dreamed about Edgar or ached for his little arms around her neck.

She did not visit as she worked. "A quiet little thing," Mrs. Stacy would say. And Mr. MacKenzie told his wife, "At least she's not always yammerin' at ya." Only Miss Dover felt concern about her silence and tried to draw her out as they sewed and mended together.

At first Damaris was reluctant to reveal anything about herself—her past, her thoughts, or her feelings—but little by little Miss Dover was able to piece together a few bits of information.

She discovered that Damaris loved to read. Miss Dover also loved to read and possessed a number of books of her own, so she was quick to suggest that Damaris might like to take a book or two home to read in the evening. Damaris could not hide the sudden light that flashed in her brown eyes.

Reading provided an opening for conversation. As Damaris returned each borrowed book, Miss Dover would smile and say, "How did you like it?" or "Who was your favorite character?" or "What did you think about" this happening or that statement?

At first Damaris answered with one or two words, but gradually she was able to express some of her thoughts and feelings about the books.

Before her first winter in the West reluctantly surrendered to a slow but tempestuous spring, Damaris had learned that whenever the words "Run on over to Miss Dover's" were spoken, her heart beat just a little bit faster. She felt comfortable and yet stimulated in the presence of the older woman.

One May afternoon Damaris ran across the street and entered the door that set the little bell to jingling. Miss Dover looked up from her sewing, her strange little glasses perched on the end of her nose.

"Hello," she said with a smile as she watched Damaris shake the spring rain from her shawl before hanging it on the coat tree. "So you got caught in the rain?"

Damaris smiled in response. "I don't mind—really. It's almost fun—like being a kid again."

Miss Dover laughed at the comment. Damaris was still little more than a kid.

"And how old are you now?" Miss Dover asked kindly.

"Goin' on sixteen. I had my fifteenth birthday on my way west."

"Have I ever told you about my trip west?" asked Miss Dover, tucking away the information about Damaris's age.

Damaris shook her head and seated herself on a stool next to Miss Dover. She reached for the mending basket that held her task for the day.

"It was a long time ago—it seems like eons. I was seventeen at the time—not much older than you. Though my eighteenth birthday was coming close.

"I had met and fallen in love with this wonderful, wonderful man. He had asked me to marry him—and Papa had given his permission. Things looked just wonderful and we had the date all set for a September wedding. And then that spring—just as the leaves were coming out—the leaves that I expected to be turning to gold and red by my wedding day— the army sent him out West. He was an army man—though he planned to settle and go into law as soon as his army days were fulfilled. But my . . ." Miss Dover stopped her needle and looked off into the distance. She sighed, then smiled at Damaris. "My, he looked handsome in his uniform," she said without embarrassment.

Damaris felt her own cheeks flush at hearing such an intimate secret.

"Well, he went on west as bidden and I stayed at home. But the closer and closer we got to that September date, the sadder and sadder I felt. Finally my papa said—my mama had already been gone for three years—'Katherine—we have two alternatives as I see it. We can have you wasting away day by day in your longings for that young man—or we can pack you up and send you west to marry as you had agreed.' I could have hugged my papa. In fact, I did.

"So it was decided. We wrote letters to Andrew and he arranged everything for my trip. Then I climbed aboard a wagon train that was taking supplies to the fort. I was the only woman in the whole train. At first I felt very uncomfortable—but I kept reminding myself that I was going to Andrew.

"It was a horrible trip. One day would be so hot that you could hardly breathe and the next would pour rain from the skies until the wheels of the wagons would be buried in the mire.

"At last we reached Fort Collins. It was wonderful to see Andrew again. He had lost weight—was very tanned. But he still looked just as handsome in his uniform. We planned our wedding all over again. We knew there would be no lovely church—no gowned attendants—no wedding feast or wedding gifts. But we didn't care. We had each other."

She stopped and looked out the nearby window as though picturing the scenes again.

"I met a nice lady who was married to one of the officers. She agreed to attend me, and Andrew had many friends among the army men, and he picked his attendant from among them."

Miss Dover roused herself in her chair before continuing. "Well, three days before the ceremony Andrew was sent out on patrol—and—well—he never came back."

Her last words tumbled out on top of one another, and Damaris wondered if she had heard correctly.

"You mean—?" she began.

Miss Dover nodded her head. "He was killed in some skirmish. I—I never asked for details."

All of the color drained from Damaris's face. She couldn't imagine going through such a terrible experience. She stared at the face of the woman before her, her thoughts in a whirl.

"And—and you never went home?" she whispered.

"I was going to. In fact, I made my arrangements with the army. I was to return with a train the next month—but then I got a notice that Papa had died. He was all I had— back home. I saw no reason for going then. I dreaded the thought of that long, dusty trip. So I asked the army to get me to the closest town, and they brought me here. I got a small inheritance from my father's estate, and I opened up this little shop. I have been here ever since. My, I guess that was over thirty years ago now."

There was silence in the room. Miss Dover seemed to have gone back in time. Damaris wondered if she was seeing the dashing young man in his army uniform or listening to the voice of her father.

Slowly Damaris began to move the needle again, in and out around the patch she was sewing on a pair of men's trousers. Soon Miss Dover stirred and the machine began to whir again. Damaris heard her speak, though her voice was little more than a whisper. "That was a long, long time ago."

Damaris said nothing.

Then Miss Dover surprised her with a sudden question. "Did you ever have a young man you cared about?"

Damaris was too embarrassed to respond at first, but finally, with flaming cheeks, she shook her head slowly. "No," she said honestly, "I never have."

"Well, you will," predicted Miss Dover. "You have most attractive eyes. Men will notice them."

Damaris shook her head slowly. She had made up her mind long ago. She had no interest in marrying—anybody, ever.

"Do you like parties?" asked Miss Dover.

"I—I don't think so," she answered.

"Well, maybe we should find out. Would you like me to have a party and—"

"Oh no," cut in Damaris, fear showing in her eyes. "I—I mean—I don't know any of the young folk of the town and—"

"But it would be a way to get to know them," went on Miss Dover.

"I—I'd rather not—really," said Damaris, her face now pale with concern.

Miss Dover let it pass, but she wondered why a pretty young girl like Damaris would have such strong feelings about parties. Instead of asking, she changed the subject.

"You have a beautiful name," she said. "I have never heard it before. Is it a family name?"

Color washed the girl's cheeks once more. She even lifted her head briefly and peeked over her needle at the older woman as she spoke.

"It's from the Bible," she said, pride coloring her voice.

"From the Bible?"

Damaris nodded again. If there was anything personal she had the slightest pride about it was her Bible name.

"We should look it up," said Miss Dover.

"You—you have a Bible?" Damaris could hardly believe the good fortune.

"Oh yes. I have a Bible. I don't know how I would ever have survived without it."

Miss Dover rose from her chair and left the sewing room for her small suite of living quarters beyond. She returned with a black book in her hand. Damaris saw that it looked just like the ones the people carried when they entered the little church back home on Sunday, all dressed in their finest clothes. It was all she could do to keep from reaching out for the book.

Miss Dover sat down and opened the Bible across her knees. "Do you know where it speaks of Damaris?" she asked.

Damaris was disappointed. She had hoped Miss Dover would be able to tell her.

She shook her head slowly. "Mama didn't say—an' we didn't have a Bible—anymore."

"Well, we'll just have to look for it then," said Miss Dover, and she closed the book, laid it aside, and returned to her sewing.

Damaris could hardly stand it. There lay the book with her name within easy reach—and she had to sit and ply her needle in and out of the tough material, sewing patches onto worn overalls.

"It has always bothered me that there is no church here," Miss Dover remarked. "That is the thing I have missed the most about home. Year after year I have prayed that God would send this town a minister—and I still pray. I believe that someday—perhaps soon—the answer will come."

Damaris did not look up. She knew that church and the
Bible book were somehow connected, but she really didn't
know just how.

"It pains me to see the children of the town growing up
without any knowledge of God," went on Miss Dover. "Why,
I never would have gotten through those difficult times had
I not had Him. I was so thankful that my mama and my papa
had given me a strong base of faith. When I couldn't understand, then I could—could just trust. I knew without doubt
that God still loved me—and He wouldn't forsake me."

Damaris had no idea what the woman was talking about.
She listened politely, making no comment, but the words
were totally foreign to her. She had, somewhere in her past,
heard references to God. She couldn't remember when or
where—oh yes, her mama had mentioned something. But
Damaris had never heard talk about trust—or about God
loving people. But then, Miss Dover was an easy person to
love. Perhaps God did love her.

The bell at the door jangled and a woman entered the
room. She was tall and straight and her stern expression
warned the world not to cross her. Damaris recognized her
as Mrs. Henry, a woman she had waited on in Mr. Mac-
Kenzie's store. At first she had been terrified of the lady. In
fact, she wondered if Mr. MacKenzie himself was not a little
frightened of her. Damaris had noticed that he was always
busy with something when Mrs. Henry entered the premises
so that Damaris had to look after the customer.

Miss Dover did not seem to mind the stern-faced lady.
She rose from her chair and smiled her warm smile. "Mrs.
Henry. Good morning. I have your things ready for you.
Right here. My, Mary must have grown. These dresses are a
good six inches longer than the last ones I sewed for her."

Mrs. Henry did not beam and speak lovingly of her growing daughter. Instead, she scowled and commented about the
child costing her a fortune with her growing spurts.

"And how is Mr. Henry? I heard he had a bout with a
chest cold."

"You heard right. He's kept me waiting on him all winter. And I had to do his share of the work besides."

"Well, now that spring is finally here," went on Miss Dover, "perhaps he will be able to shake the illness and regain his strength."

"I certainly hope so," the woman retorted. "I've had about all I can take. And now the spring work is starting, I have no intention of shouldering that burden all alone."

She gathered her sewn dresses for Mary, paid her bill with some grumbling, and left without a "good-day."

"Well," Miss Dover sighed after the door had closed, "they say it takes all kinds of people to make our world, but I often wonder just what it is that shapes them into what they are. Now take Mrs. Henry—what do you suppose has happened in her past to make her so—so sad and troubled all the time?"

Damaris thought about repeating what Mr. MacKenzie had said, that she was a sour old buzzard—out looking for someone's bones to pick. But she held her tongue.

"People like her need extra kindness," Miss Dover said. "Just think of the pain she must have buried inside."

Damaris had never thought about such things before. She had always taken people at face value, never trying to figure out the reasons for their behavior. It was difficult for her just to serve Mrs. Henry without making her more upset. Damaris always sighed with relief when the woman was finally out the door. Miss Dover seemed to feel it her duty to try to understand the woman and apply some healing balm to whatever was hurting her.

It was all strange to Damaris. She didn't know what made Miss Dover so kind any more than she knew what made Mrs. Henry so mean—but she was glad to be able to spend some of her time at the kind woman's little shop.

Chapter Twelve

The Book

"Would you like to borrow a Bible?" asked Miss Dover when Damaris wrapped her shawl around her shoulders and prepared to run back through the light rain to help Mrs. Stacy.

Damaris was so caught by surprise that she could not even answer.

Miss Dover must have seen the light in her eyes. "I can't spare mine," she said, "but Papa's is here. You may borrow it if you wish."

She left Damaris standing while she went to get it.

Damaris knew the Bible must be precious to Miss Dover. "I'll take special care of it," she promised, tucking it under her shawl away from the rain.

Miss Dover nodded and smiled. "I'm sure you will."

Damaris rushed home. She could scarcely bear the thought of laying the book in her room until she had completed her tasks. If only she could crawl off by herself and curl up and read and read until she discovered the story about the woman named Damaris.

But she had work to do. The boarders had to be fed. The guests had to be served. There was wood and water to haul. Dishes to do. Floors to sweep. The list went on and on.

At last Damaris finished her work and put aside her apron. She could still hear the voices of Mrs. Stacy and Mr. Hebert from the dining room. Whenever Mr. Hebert came to town, it meant more duties for Damaris because Mrs. Stacy would sit and chat and laugh with the gentleman, leaving Damaris alone to do the dishes and clean up.

Damaris no longer needed to wait for Mrs. Stacy to give leave for her to go to her room. She knew each task that needed to be cared for, and as soon as it was accomplished, she was free to retire.

She hurriedly removed her day clothes and climbed into Miss Dover's hand-me-down flannel nightie. Then she checked her lamp to be sure it had lots of oil, snuggled down under her blankets, and gently picked up the worn Bible of Miss Dover's papa.

She turned the first few pages, past the inscription of King James, past the table of contents, and on to a page that bore the title "Genesis." It looked to Damaris that this was the place to begin. She snuggled down against her pillow, eager to get started.

It was a strange story. All about God creating things. Damaris had wondered how everything had come into existence. Then God made man—and that seemed to be a mistake. But Damaris read on.

The door slammed as Mr. Hebert took his leave. Damaris wondered briefly why the man had chosen to ride on home with the drizzling rain still falling. She turned back to the pages. What Mr. Hebert chose to do was of little concern to her.

Then she heard Mrs. Stacy moving about the house, checking this and locking that. At last the steps retreated and Damaris heard a door close softly.

Still Damaris read on. The book was filled with many stories but no mention of Damaris. Damaris was disappointed, but she continued reading. She was bound to find her story if she read far enough.

She read of a flood that covered the whole earth. Only a few people survived. She wondered what it would have been like to be shut up in the big boat with all the animals. Damaris decided that she would have liked it. She had always preferred animals to people.

She read of Joseph—the boy who was sold by his brothers. Damaris felt anger and hate fill her whole being. When the brothers went to Egypt to buy grain, Damaris read more quickly. Now Joseph could get even for what they had done to him. But instead he forgave them. She couldn't understand his response.

The hall clock kept ticking and Damaris kept reading. Still no sign of "Damaris." The stories kept drawing her on, but she'd had a long, busy day. Her eyelids started to droop. She could read no further.

As the Bible began to slip from her fingers, Damaris jerked to attention. She mustn't drop the book. She placed it carefully in the drawer in the stand beside her bed. Then she blew out her light, snuggled down under the covers once more, and let her eyes close.

"I didn't find her," she murmured to herself. "I didn't find her. All of those people—and no Damaris."

———

Damaris was beginning to put the townspeople's names and faces together. Her three part-time jobs helped her do the matching. If she didn't see them in the dining room at Mrs. Stacy's boardinghouse, she might see them picking up mending or new garments at Miss Dover's sewing room. And if she didn't see them at either of those places, she was almost sure to serve them at some time at Mr. MacKenzie's store.

Even though Damaris could name almost everyone in the community, she really could claim none as her friends—with perhaps the exception of Miss Dover.

Mr. MacKenzie, though kind enough to Damaris, could be gruff and curt. Damaris took and obeyed orders and stayed as far away from the store owner as space would allow. Mrs. Stacy was nice enough, but she did seem to take advantage of Damaris. She obviously realized she had made herself a very good deal. Damaris worked hard and well, ate little, and demanded nothing. Mrs. Stacy had far more time to socialize than ever before, which was particularly enjoyable when Mr. Hebert came to town.

Miss Dover was gentle and kind. She dressed simply yet neatly. She spoke words of kindness wherever she went. Men always doffed their hats and women always smiled a good morning, and even children grinned and pressed a little closer when Miss Dover walked the streets. She was to Damaris everything that a true lady should be. Without realizing it, Damaris tried to pattern her own conduct after that of Miss Dover.

The kind woman seemed to genuinely enjoy Damaris's company and expressed interest in all her employee was doing. Damaris could not understand or explain why, but she felt comfortable with Miss Dover—as though a very important part of herself was able to function—to exist—in the presence of the older woman.

So Damaris spent her days rushing through duties at the boardinghouse and the store so she could run breathlessly across the street, slide into a chair beside her mending basket, and enjoy Miss Dover's presence.

On one such day, Damaris took her place and reached for her needle and an item of mending.

"What are you reading now?" Miss Dover asked. The Bible had become a usual topic of their conversation.

"About King David," answered Damaris, lifting her eyes from her work for a moment.

"Ah—King David. He is one of my favorite Bible characters. If I had ever been blessed with a son, I would have called him David."

Miss Dover sighed. Damaris imagined that the memory of her lost love must still cause her pain.

"Do you like him?" Miss Dover asked, turning their thoughts to the Bible David again.

Damaris was still a bit uneasy expressing her thoughts and feelings, but Miss Dover continued to draw her out little by little.

"I—I guess so," Damaris answered slowly.

"Oh, I love him!" Miss Dover exclaimed. "He was so—so full of life—of feeling—of—of love," she said, using her plump hand to express the depth of her emotions.

Damaris looked up from her sewing with eyes wide with wonder.

"You don't feel that?" asked Miss Dover, noticing the girl's surprise.

Damaris wished to agree. She even nodded her head slightly. But then she dared to say, in almost a whisper, "He did some pretty bad things."

Miss Dover smiled. "Ah, yes. He did. He certainly did. But he was so repentant. So deeply troubled by his sin. He cried out to God with such remorse."

Damaris held her sewing needle still a moment as she contemplated Miss Dover's comment.

"That is what really counts," said Miss Dover. "Not all the foolish mistakes we make, though we should certainly seek the will of God before we make a move—not after—so that we need not make such terrible mistakes in the first place; but if we do make mistakes, then we must be remorseful. Repentant. We must ask for forgiveness. God will forgive if we confess our sin."

Damaris had never heard such strange talk.

"Before you go, I will give you some verses to read. The Psalms show us so much about David. About the way he prayed for forgiveness. And how God forgave him. Why, even in the New Testament, there are verses where God talks about 'my David' just as though David had never committed a sin in his entire life. Isn't that amazing?"

Damaris nodded, but she wasn't sure as to what she was agreeing.

"And Jonathan. My, I love Jonathan. I think I would have named my son David Jonathan. Or Jonathan David—I was never quite sure. Well, for a king's son—a young prince—Jonathan was the most unselfish, the most unspoiled young man. My! I admire Jonathan."

The bell jangled and a young man stepped slowly into the room. When Miss Dover saw who it was, she rose quickly from her chair, a smile flooding her face.

"Gil!" she exclaimed, pleasure softening her voice. "Oh, Gil, it's so good to see you. Why, I thought you must have been storm-bound in that valley of yours. Haven't seen you for months and months."

The young man chuckled. "Truth is, I spent part of the winter down south. I was roundin' up a few more head of good stock. The offer came up unexpectedly, so there wasn't an opportunity to let you know I'd be gone."

"Then you are forgiven," said Miss Dover, drawing closer to the young man. "I feared that you had just forgotten me."

"Now, Miss Dover," said the voice with the slight drawl, "you know right well I'd never be doin' that."

Then the talk took a more serious tone.

"How have you been?" asked Miss Dover with real concern. "Did you find the stock you wanted?"

"I did. Could hardly wait to get them back here on my own spread. Got some new spring calves already. Prettiest little things you ever saw."

"Oh, Gil, it's so good to see you. And I'm so relieved to know you're well. Please come in so we can catch up a bit."

Damaris was noticing something different about Miss Dover's conversation with the young man. A warmth, an intimacy.

"Have you met Damaris?" asked Miss Dover suddenly. "No, of course you haven't," she quickly added. "She came in the fall. She's been working for me."

Damaris dreaded introductions, especially to men. She always felt so awkward.

"Damaris Withers, this is Gilwyn Lewis. He owns a ranch back in the hills. But he does manage to get to town now and then," Miss Dovers teased.

Damaris looked up long enough to nod her head and mumble, "Pleased to meet you." Then she quickly lowered her eyes again.

She wasn't sure what she had seen. Just a tall, rugged young man with longish, slightly curling brown hair—and sharp blue eyes that in one brief glance seemed to pierce clear through to her soul.

Damaris felt uncomfortable, and the color rose in her cheeks. She turned slightly, to put her back to the gentleman, and thrust her needle into her work so quickly that she pricked her finger.

"Can you stay for coffee?" Miss Dover was asking. "I'd love to hear about your winter."

"I'd like that," agreed the young man as he tossed his dusty, weathered Stetson into the corner and moved forward.

"Damaris, would you like to join us?" asked Miss Dover.

Damaris knew she would never be able to move from her chair in the presence of this stranger. She wasn't even sure she would be able to speak. She started to shake her head. That much she could manage. She was surprised to hear her own voice say, "I don't have long. I think I'd better finish this patch."

Miss Dover accepted her decision without further comment.

Damaris could hear the rattle of coffee cups, an occasional laugh, and the drone of conversation, but she could not make out any of the words.

She finished her patch as quickly as she could and stood to brush the threads from her skirts. She would run on back to Mrs. Stacy's in plenty of time to help with the evening meal.

As she moved to the door, intending to leave as quickly and quietly as she could, she remembered Miss Dover's promise about the verses in Psalms. She was eager to read them. Perhaps they would help her understand David's story better. But there was no opportunity to get them now. Damaris would never have interrupted the conversation beyond the dividing door. She would just have to wait for the references until another time.

Damaris was just wrapping her shawl around her shoulders when Miss Dover came into the room.

"I thought I heard you leaving," she said. "I haven't given you the scriptures. Here, I've written them down. I may think of more later, but this will give you a start."

Damaris murmured her thanks and turned to go, but Miss Dover put a hand lightly on her arm. "What do you think of Gil?" she whispered.

Damaris didn't have an answer ready.

Miss Dover seemed not to mind. Perhaps she hadn't really expected one. A warm gleam lighted her eyes. "I'll tell you about him sometime," she promised. "He's—he's my David Jonathan."

Chapter Thirteen

Confusion

Damaris hurried to carry in the wood and water, for Mrs. Stacy was already working in the big kitchen preparing the evening meal. Damaris knew all of the boarders by name—though she never called them by such except when speaking with Mrs. Stacy. Damaris served them, as quietly and efficiently as she could, then moved on, careful not to be involved in any type of conversation.

For the most part, she did not mind the job, but on one occasion she was more than thankful that the sheriff was a live-in at the boardinghouse. Most town drinkers knew that Sheriff Gordon took his meals at Mrs. Stacy's. Damaris had often smelled whiskey as men entered the dining room and took their places. It never failed to make her quake and wish to flee the room. But she gradually had come to realize not all men drank until their money was totally gone. Unlike her pa, these men with whiskey on their breath still had enough to pay for their supper, and often tucked even more money back into their pockets. And never did they drink so much as to be troublesome—except one time. Damaris recalled that evening as she did her chores. No matter how hard she tried to dismiss it from her memory, it always came back.

Damaris had smelled whiskey the minute the fellow entered. He was a stranger, so perhaps he didn't know that the sheriff was sitting at the corner table facing the door, right where he always sat.

"Look after the gentleman over there," Mrs. Stacy said, nodding toward the stranger.

Damaris trembled. She had been taught to be obedient, so she moved forward as bidden, but her whole body tensed to meet whatever assault might greet her.

At first the man seemed quiet, and Damaris hoped that he'd had enough to drink to already make him drowsy and in a stupor.

"Can I help you?" she asked, unable to bring herself to add "sir," as she had been taught.

He mumbled something in reply without looking up.

"Can I help you?" Damaris asked a little louder.

"Wha-a?" he asked with a slurred voice. Then he lifted his head and stared at Damaris.

Damaris felt her body lean back, but her feet did not move.

"Would you like—?" she began, but the man grasped her wrist with his dirty hand.

"Yeah—I'd like—" he sneered.

Before he finished his sentence, the sheriff was standing beside Damaris, his shiny badge flashing conspicuously on his leather vest.

"Mister," Damaris heard the sheriff say in a cold, menacing voice she had never heard him use before, "I don't think ya really want to eat here tonight."

Each word was slow and deliberate. The sheriff's eyes drilled into the red eyes of the man at the table, pinning him to the spot.

The grip on Damaris's hand gradually relaxed and the man drew back his hand.

"Weren't meanin' no harm," the man grumbled. "Fella can't even have any fun." But he did not argue further.

He stumbled from the room, and the sheriff returned to his table. Damaris shifted uncomfortably, feeling that all eyes were upon her. More than her wrist was stinging from the assault.

"Here's my plate. I'm done," said the sheriff. "Why don't ya start washin' up."

Damaris reached for the sheriff's plate and took the opportunity to flee the room. When she reached the kitchen she placed the plate on the worktable and leaned her head against the coolness of the windowpane. She wished she never had to serve tables again.

At last her quaking lessened enough for her to pick up the plate and move toward the dishpan of hot water. The sheriff had eaten only half of his meal. Damaris knew his eating habits well enough to know that he always cleaned his plate, then wiped up the last particles with a swab of bread. She was puzzled, but she would rather try to forget the incident than understand it. Damaris tried to dismiss it, but she could not help but think of it each time a new man came to the dining room.

The thought of a new man brought her mind back to the present. As she went about her serving duties she recalled the young man she had just met at Miss Dover's. What were his drinking habits? Would he be draining a bottle at the local saloon and then coming to Mrs. Stacy's for supper?

Then she thought of Miss Dover's shining eyes and whispered words, "He is my 'David Jonathan.' " What had she meant by the remark? David Jonathan was the name she said she had picked for a son. Did Miss Dover mean that the young man was her son? No, that was unthinkable. She had said, "If I had ever had a son I would have called him David Jonathan." Miss Dover had never had opportunity to use the name.

What did she mean? Was the young man like a son to her? Damaris decided that was probably the case. With that thought came some relief. Damaris felt quite confident that Miss Dover would expect a son of hers to control his drinking—even if he did come to town with money in his pocket.

Then Damaris recalled how uneasy the young man's

piercing blue eyes had made her feel, and she hoped he would make no appearance at all.

The meal began as usual. All of the regulars took their seats, and Damaris and Mrs. Stacy were both kept busy caring for them. Two farmers also joined the group. Damaris had seen them on a few occasions before.

Damaris hurried to the kitchen with a stack of dirty plates. When she returned with a tray of saskatoon pie, she saw that another guest had entered the room.

Mrs. Stacy stepped back and reached out her hand to Damaris.

"I'll take that pie," she said. "You get a plate of supper for Gil." Then she added, loudly enough for everyone to hear, "An' heap it high. That boy's got a real appetite."

Everyone in the room joined in the laughter.

Damaris spun on her heel and headed back to the kitchen. There was no way she was ready to look into those blue eyes again. Her hand trembled as she sliced off roast beef and piled mashed potatoes on a clean plate. She spooned the gravy over the whole thing, added some creamed carrots, and took a deep breath to steel herself for carrying the plate into the dining room.

The man was still the center of conversation. He hadn't even made his way to a table yet. Damaris moved to where there was an empty chair, set the plate down, and turned away. That was easy. She hadn't needed to say one word— or even look at him.

"More coffee, Damaris," instructed Mrs. Stacy, and Damaris hurried to the kitchen for the large pot.

Her hand shook as she poured. She hoped she would not embarrass herself by spilling it. Making her way around the tables, she carefully refilled cup after cup.

"Could I have a cup, too, please," a soft yet husky voice requested. Damaris recognized it as belonging to Miss Dover's Gil.

She moved closer to reach for his cup. As she poured the hot liquid, she could feel his eyes upon her, but she refused to meet his gaze.

"I thought you worked for Miss Dover," he said softly.

"I do," said Damaris with no further explanation. She replaced the full cup on the table and moved on, relieved that she still had not had to meet his eyes.

She returned to the kitchen and placed the nearly empty pot back on the stove. Her body trembled slightly, but she could not understand why. What had he done to frighten her so?

Then a new thought came to her. She had stood near his chair as she had poured the coffee and had smelled no liquor at all.

———

The next morning as Damaris sorted a new batch of yard goods at the store, she heard the sound of squeaking door hinges and footsteps crossing the floor. She lifted her head and turned to help the customer who had entered. Her breath caught in her throat, and she stopped stock-still when she saw who it was.

Her slight movement drew his attention, and Gil turned to her, a smile already on his face. Upon recognizing her his smile was quickly replaced by a look of confusion. Then a slow grin began to turn up the corners of his mouth and cause those deep blue eyes to twinkle.

"Well, I'll be!" he laughed. "You runnin' this town? I'm surprised the sheriff still has his badge."

Damaris knew he was teasing her. She flushed, her eyes dropping quickly, the hint of a smile showing on her lips.

"Guess it must look that way," she admitted, moving toward the counter. "Fact is, I have three jobs—all part time."

She became businesslike then. "You need supplies?" she asked as she moved behind the counter, picking up a small notebook in which to write accounts.

"I sure do," he said, moving forward. "I seem to be out of everything back at the ranch." He fumbled in a shirt pocket. "Here," he said, handing her a small sheet of paper. "I've got it all written down on this list."

Damaris took the paper and scanned the items. It made

her job so much simpler when customers came in prepared.
Some of them stood there half the morning thinking and
scratching their heads and trying to remember, then making
up their minds and changing them again. Damaris was always relieved to see a list.

"If you have something else to do, I'll work on this and
have it ready for you in about half an hour," said Damaris
as she reached for a bag of salt.

"No," he replied, much to her dismay. "I've already looked
after everything else. I'm anxious now to collect my supplies
and get on back to the ranch. I'll mosey around here and see
if I've forgotten anything."

Damaris moved as quickly as she could, gathering the
items one by one and piling them on the counter. Now and
then he commented about something or took a heavy item
from her hands.

"How you liking Dixen?" he asked.

"It's okay," Damaris answered without feeling or convic-
tion.

She hurried to get his pail of lard.

"Plannin' to stay?" he probed.

Damaris wasn't sure if he was nosey or just trying to
make polite conversation.

"Guess so," she said carelessly.

Damaris placed the last grocery item on the counter and
began adding up the total cost.

"Oh, I forgot," he said. "I need some nails. I tried at the
hardware across the way but they were all out. MacKenzie
got any here?"

"What kind of nails?" asked Damaris. "We have three
sizes."

Damaris found it unnerving to walk by his side as they
went together to look at the nails.

He chose the ones he wanted and Damaris measured the
amount. She was more anxious than he to have the order
filled and to get him on his way back to his ranch.

He laid the money on the counter and began to carry
boxes and sacks to the waiting wagon.

"See you again," he called to Damaris as he shouldered the large sack of flour as though it were a mere ten-pound bag of sugar and took his leave.

Damaris ran a trembling hand over her hair. She had thought him gone—for good. But now he was reminding her that this was his town. He came to this store for his supplies. He stopped to eat his meals at Mrs. Stacy's boardinghouse. And he seemed to be on some kind of special terms with Miss Dover. Yes, she realized. She was likely—very likely—to see him again. She wished she could figure out why he made her so uneasy. Perhaps if she understood, she could cope with it better.

Chapter Fourteen

Time

Tomorrow is my birthday, noted Damaris as she looked at the calendar posted on the wall in Mrs. Stacy's kitchen.

She felt neither sadness nor excitement. Only surprise that it had been over a year since she left home.

Usually she pushed thoughts of home from her mind whenever they came to her. Now, as she stood looking at the calendar, she let her mind stop long enough to wonder how things were with her mama. She knew her birthday would be in Mama's thinking.

"I'll be sixteen," she whispered. "Sixteen," she said again. "One more year 'til I'm seventeen. Mama said a girl should be ready to be on her own by then."

I wish Mama knew that I'm fine, her thoughts continued. "I wish she could see my new dresses and my new shoes," she murmured, "and that I even have more money on my account at the store. Maybe I'll even have enough to get me some real winter high-tops." Damaris had admired the boots as she unpacked them and placed them on the shelves.

"Or maybe a coat—instead of my shawl. Shawls are hard to hold in place on a windy day."

Damaris heard a step on the porch and closed her mouth. Mrs. Stacy was returning from her call. Damaris turned from the calendar. Tomorrow would come and go like any other day.

———

One day in early fall Damaris lifted her eyes to see Mr. Brown standing at the counter. She had come to think that the family had completely disappeared from her life.

At the sight of him, Damaris felt her heart leap. Edgar! It had been so long since she had seen Edgar.

She moved forward eagerly to greet the man and see the small boy.

"Hello, Damaris," he said, his eyes brightening. "You're lookin' well. Had a good first year?"

Damaris nodded, surprised at how shy she suddenly felt. "And you?" she asked.

"For the most part," he said, but his eyes darkened before his head lowered.

Fear tightened Damaris's stomach. Something had happened. Was it Edgar? She dared not ask.

"How is Mrs. Brown?" she finally said.

"She's keepin' well. Fair. She's to have another child soon."

Damaris thought of the frail woman with her arms already filled with fussing babies and wondered how she would ever manage with another one.

"Does—does she have some place to go?" Damaris asked with hesitation.

"A neighbor woman has promised to come. She's delivered lots of babies. It'll be fine. Mrs. Brown has never had trouble."

Damaris wondered if he felt as sure as he tried to sound.

"And the—the children?" she said at last.

His eyes darkened again. She knew it. She knew it. Her heart constricted within her chest. She should have kept Edgar with her. Somehow. She should not have left him. She should have found some way to see that they were never separated.

"Edgar still talks of you," Mr. Brown finally said.

Damaris looked up quickly, her wildly beating heart giving an extra thud.

"How is he?" she managed to say in spite of her dry mouth.

"Growin' like a weed," said Mr. Brown. He smiled for the first time. "Goin' to be drivin' a team before we know it."

Damaris felt weak with relief.

"And the others?" she asked.

"We buried the wee one," replied Mr. Brown, disclosing the reason for the pain in his eyes.

"I'm—I'm sorry," she whispered.

"Never was right," went on Mr. Brown as though he was glad to have someone who would understand his grief. "Always fussy and sickly. Never gained like he shoulda. Nearly wore Mrs. Brown out. Thought fer sure things would right themselves once we settled—but he jest seemed to git worse and worse."

"When?" asked Damaris.

"Jest afore Christmas."

Damaris couldn't speak further. She was relieved when Mr. Brown turned the conversation to his purchases.

"We're only a little further from Dixen than we are from Casey," he explained. "I've been goin' on over there fer supplies an' then my neighbor fella says thet things are sometimes a bit cheaper over here, so I decided to check it out myself."

Damaris nodded.

"From lookin' round at the prices—I think he's right. Might be comin' this way from now on."

Damaris felt excitement creep over her. She might get to see Edgar again. When she had finished filling the order, she scooped a handful of gumdrops into a little brown bag and handed them to Mr. Brown.

"For the children," she explained. "From me. Tell them I still think of them. And—and give my regards to Mrs. Brown."

The man smiled and thanked her. Then he hoisted the remainder of groceries onto his shoulder and left the store. Damaris lifted a hand to bid farewell and then turned to write the candy on her account card.

Mr. Brown continued to come to their store about once a month for some time after that, but he didn't bring Edgar with him. He did, however, bring news of a new baby girl.

"I was hoping fer another boy," he admitted to Damaris. "Fella can never have too many hands to help with the work."

Damaris thought of Mrs. Brown. Surely she could use a few hands as well. Then, remembering the couple's rather spoiled, carefree daughters, Damaris wondered if Mrs. Brown would have help no matter how many girls she had.

Damaris tucked in a little gift for the new baby along with the candy she always sent to the children. The purchases made a bit of a hole in her money on account, but Damaris refused to mope about it.

"Tell Mrs. Brown I am happy for her," she said.

Mr. Brown nodded as he left and promised to carry the message.

———

Damaris also saw Gil now and then. He didn't come to town often, and when he did he always seemed to be in a hurry. Damaris avoided him if she could, feigning busyness at the store or kitchen duties at the boardinghouse. It was not so easy to escape his presence at Miss Dover's. He always took time to call on the town seamstress, even though he did not have sewing or mending to be done. If Damaris happened to be working, he greeted her as well; but he did not linger to chat, and Damaris was glad about that.

———

Winter came in with a chill wind, gripping icy fingers on exposed hands and cheeks. Damaris had to choose between the boots and the coat and finally decided on the boots. She could wrap her heavy shawl around her for another season. She didn't have to travel far anyway, but it would be nice to have high-top boots when crossing snowdrifts between places of employment.

One day as Damaris pushed open Miss Dover's door, a blast of wind caught the bell, causing it to jingle wildly. She closed the door as quickly as she could to shut out the weather and shook the snow from her hair and shawl.

"My," said Miss Dover, "I had no idea it was that nasty. You shouldn't have come."

"It's not that bad," answered Damaris. She thought, but didn't add, that she would have braved much worse weather and traveled a much greater distance to enjoy the woman's companionship.

"I think we'll need to light the lamp," said Miss Dover. "It has become quite dark."

Damaris nodded and went to light it. She wished that she could stand for a few minutes with her fingers wrapped around the warm globe. How cold her hands had become in the short distance! She had not been able to tuck them underneath her shawl because the wind would have stolen away her wrap if she had not held on to it tightly with both hands.

"I think it's about time for you to learn to use the machine," said Miss Dover.

Damaris jerked to attention.

"Are you interested?"

Damaris had dreamed of using the machine. Whenever she looked up from her own mending, she studied the hands of Miss Dover as they skillfully guided the material under the foot that cradled the needle.

"I'd—I'd love to if you think—"

"I'm sure you'll catch on in no time," Miss Dover assured her.

Damaris forgot all about her cold fingers and followed Miss Dover to the machine.

The day went all too quickly. Damaris was a good student and was soon enjoying the thrill of seeing finished seams turn out under her guiding hand. Her eyes, hands, and feet worked in unison, producing an even stitch.

"It's just as I thought," said Miss Dover with a pleased voice. "You are a natural seamstress."

Damaris flushed at the praise. She so much wanted to be like Miss Dover. She worked on, her eyes fastened on the cloth.

All too soon it was time for her to put away her sewing and hurry across the street to help Mrs. Stacy again. She laid aside the unfinished garment and wrapped her shawl firmly around her shoulders.

"How is your reading coming?" Miss Dover asked just as Damaris was ready to leave. "Where are you now?"

"I'm reading the—the story of—well, it's not a story really. It's the—the book of Ezekiel."

"Oh," said Miss Dover thoughtfully. "Are you enjoying it?"

Damaris hardly knew how to answer. She looked down at her new high-top boots. Already they were showing a faint scuff on one toe. She wanted to bend down and polish it with the end of her shawl, but she decided to wait until she was alone in her room.

"Well—I don't much understand it," she admitted. "All of the—the woes and—and pretendings."

"Pretendings? Oh, you mean visions? Well, I admit that there is much of it that I don't understand, either."

Damaris placed a hand on the door handle. She had to go. Mrs. Stacy would be impatient if she was late.

"Why don't you read from the New Testament?" suggested Miss Dover.

"Well I—I—haven't finished the Old Testament, and I—I still haven't—found my name."

Surprise showed on Miss Dover's face. Damaris was sure she had forgotten all about the name.

"Your name? Yes. Yes, we meant to look for your name." Her brow puckered slightly and she appeared to be deep in thought. "It's funny," she said, shaking her head, a smile playing about her lips. "I thought I knew my Bible pretty well, but I can't remember a story about Damaris."

Disappointment seeped to the deepest part of Damaris's being.

Then Miss Dover brightened. "But I'll help you find it,"

she promised, "and this time I won't forget." Seeing the look of relief on Damaris's face, she hurried on. "But you start in the New Testament," she said. "I think you will understand it better. I'll finish looking for your name in the Old Testament. From Ezekiel, you say?"

Damaris nodded.

"Well, then, I'll work on Ezekiel."

Damaris voiced her thanks and went back out into the swirling snow. Perhaps with both of them working on it, they would soon find the story of the Bible woman named Damaris.

Chapter Fifteen

A Dinner Guest

Damaris had enjoyed the stories in the Old Testament, but much of the "in-between," as she thought of it, left her confused. But the books of Matthew, Mark, Luke, and John were filled with exciting tales. Instead of going on to Acts, she flipped back to Matthew and began to read again. Reading the Bible was new to her, so she had to read the stories again and again to understand them. She could hardly wait for night to come so she could cuddle down in her warm bed, her head propped up on pillows and her knees drawn up to hold the book.

She loved many of the characters of the stories, but the man Jesus drew her like no other. He was different from any man she had ever known. She brushed away tears as she read of the birth in a cattle shed, with no bed for Him but a cow's manger. She could picture it in her mind from memories of her family's farm. She exulted as He walked the dusty roads speaking words of peace and healing the sick. She chuckled with glee when He put down the proud Pharisees who tried to trick Him with their questions. And she agonized as He was sentenced to death and forced to drag His cross through the streets of the city to Golgotha.

When she came at last to the story of the open tomb, Damaris hugged her knees and choked back the words she wished to say out loud. It was all so exciting, so perfect. She had never read another story quite like it.

"I wish He had really lived. I wish He had lived right here in Dixen."

At last, here was a man Damaris felt she could trust. Oh, it was true that Mr. Brown had never been harsh with her—but she had always wondered what might happen if he put a bottle to his lips. And it was true that the captain had been more than kind in finding her work, but she had been careful not to anger him. It was true too that Mr. MacKenzie was decent enough, but Damaris had smelled whiskey on his breath once or twice and feared what might happen if one day he had more money in his pocket than he knew what to do with. And it was also true that Miss Dover's Gil was always kind, but he paid little more attention to Damaris than she did to him. But with the man in the book—this Jesus—Damaris could find no reason not to trust this man.

———

Mrs. Stacy began to talk of a Christmas party again. Damaris tightened up at the thought. She would do just as she had done the year before, she decided. Mrs. Stacy hadn't questioned her much—and she *had* felt sick. Her story had not been a lie.

And then, just two days before Christmas, Miss Dover came to call on Mrs. Stacy. They visited over cups of tea for a few minutes as Damaris worked about the room. Then she heard Miss Dover ask, as calmly as you please, "I was wondering if Damaris might have Christmas Day off. I would like to have her join me for dinner."

Mrs. Stacy squirmed in her chair before she gave her answer, and Damaris held her breath. She knew that the woman really counted on her help.

"For the whole day?" asked Mrs. Stacy, making a single day sound awfully long.

"She hasn't had a day off for ever so long," continued Miss Dover, and Mrs. Stacy nodded rather reluctantly. The fact was, Damaris had never had a day off—not since she had reached their little town.

Damaris had no idea what a day off was, nor what to do

with one if she had it, but if it allowed her to spend more time at Miss Dover's house, she would be in favor of it.

"Would you like that, Damaris?" Mrs. Stacy swiveled in her chair to ask.

Damaris tried not to appear too eager. "I guess so," she said, trying to still the hammering of her heart. She wondered what special task Miss Dover had for her, but she didn't really care. She was willing to sew or mend or scrub or anything.

"Then it is settled," beamed Miss Dover. "We will plan dinner for one o'clock, but you can come as early in the morning as you wish."

Damaris thought she understood then. Miss Dover was having guests and needed help preparing dinner. It suited Damaris just fine. She nodded her head and tried to hide her pleasure.

———

Damaris was up early on Christmas Day. She had decided she wouldn't leave until she had helped Mrs. Stacy with breakfast and washed the dishes. But everyone seemed to be reluctant to climb from their beds. The guests straggled into the dining room, one by one, and Damaris soon ran out of patience.

"Why is everyone so slow this morning?" she asked Mrs. Stacy.

"Oh, on Christmas everyone likes to loaf a bit," replied the lady, seeming not to mind in the least.

"They'll be late for work," said Damaris.

"Oh, no one works on Christmas," Mrs. Stacy returned. "None of the shops will be open."

It was news to Damaris. She had paid no attention to the shops her first year in town.

"You run along," said Mrs. Stacy good-naturedly. "Ah, but before you go, I have a little gift for you."

Mrs. Stacy left the room and came back with a small package. "Here," she said. "I hope you like it. Merry Christmas."

Damaris opened the package and found a lace handker-
chief. Her eyes widened. She couldn't understand why Mrs.
Stacy had given her the gift.

"But why—?"

"It's Christmas," said the woman. "People give gifts at
Christmas."

Damaris had not received a Christmas gift since her
mama stopped giving them when Damaris reached age
seven. She assumed that such things were no longer done—
at least not for anyone past childhood.

"But—but you never—" Damaris stopped. To continue
her statement would have sounded like criticism when instead it was simply confusion.

"Last year I wasn't thinking," the woman admitted.
"None of us were thinking. We talked of it later and all felt
terrible—but it was too late to go back and do something
about it."

Damaris had no idea what Mrs. Stacy was talking about.

"But I—does everybody give gifts?"

"To family—and special friends," Mrs. Stacy answered.

"But I don't have gifts," said Damaris. "Not for anyone."
Her head was whirling. Who were her special friends? Well,
Miss Dover, certainly. And she supposed, especially as she
stood with the hankie in her hand, that Mrs. Stacy was also
a special friend. Edgar was one—but he was miles away, and
the captain had been—well, rather special, but she had no
idea where he was.

"I—I thank you," Damaris finally managed to stammer.
"It is a most pretty hankie. Too pretty to use—even to wipe
one's brow."

Mrs. Stacy smiled at the comment. "Run along now," she
said. "I'll manage just fine."

Damaris returned to her room to lay the hankie tenderly
in the little drawer of her night stand. Then she reached for
her shawl and laced on her high-top boots. As she worked
she made up her mind. She would run down the street to Mr.
MacKenzie's store. Even if it was Christmas, she was sure
he would let her in to do some picking from the stock on the

shelves. She had to have a gift for Mrs. Stacy and Miss Dover. She just had to. She had money on her account. She had been hoarding it for a new summer bonnet. She had unpacked a number of attractive ones and placed them on a shelf. Now that she was older, it was quite improper for her to be out on the streets without a hat on her head. Damaris cringed as she thought of the account money and the need for gifts. Then her chin lifted. "I'll just do without the bonnet for a bit longer," she told herself and rushed through the cold December morning to rap on the MacKenzie door.

———————

When Damaris reached Miss Dover's house, a card of shining new needles clutched firmly in her hand, she was surprised to be ushered directly to the rooms at the back.

"Merry Christmas, Damaris," said Miss Dover.

Damaris thrust forward her small gift. "For you," she said. "For Christmas."

Miss Dover fussed over the gift until Damaris flushed with embarrassment.

Then Miss Dover turned to a little cupboard and drew forth a package.

"And I have a gift for you," she said. "It isn't exactly new—in fact, it isn't new at all—but I have redesigned it. It's a bit summery, I'm afraid, but perhaps by next winter you will have a brand new one picked out from—"

Miss Dover was cut short by Damaris's squeal of delight. It was a bonnet. A bonnet far prettier than any Damaris had unpacked at the store. The young girl who so carefully guarded all thoughts and feelings could not hide her pleasure with the gift.

"Oh, Miss Dover. It's—it's lovely," she managed to say, and her eyes told just how much she meant the words.

"I'm pleased you like it," said Miss Dover. "The color will suit you beautifully."

Damaris looked again at the soft cream material. Pretty bows clustered against the sloping brim and a large feather plume swept gracefully up one side and over the top.

"We must sew a dress to go with it," said Miss Dover and then amended her statement. "You can sew it yourself on the machine—perhaps in the evenings when your other work is done."

Damaris couldn't imagine a dress beautiful enough to compliment the wonderful bonnet. Suddenly she realized that she should have been assuming her household chores instead of standing there admiring her new hat. She placed the hat lovingly back in its box and turned to Miss Dover.

"What do you wish me to do?" she asked. Already the rooms were filled with delicious odors.

"All is done—for the moment," said the woman. "Why don't we just sit down and chat 'til our other guest arrives."

At the surprised look on Damaris's face, Miss Dover explained, "Gil is coming for dinner, too. But he won't be here until a bit later. He had things to do in the morning and it is rather a long ride, I'm afraid. But he promised he'd be here as soon as he could."

Damaris panicked. She hadn't realized that she would be asked to serve Gil.

"Now, why don't you run on home and put on your prettiest dress. The one we made you last summer. Why, I have scarcely seen you wear it."

Damaris hesitated. The dress was special to her. She hated to get it spotted with grease or spatterings.

"If we should clean-up together later," Miss Dover went on, "I promise that I'll give you an ample, heavy apron to cover it completely. But as my guest, I want you to feel ladylike and lovely."

"Your guest?" Damaris could not stop the words.

"You didn't know you were to be my guest? Why, yes. For Christmas dinner. You and Gil. The two people dearest to me."

Damaris stood still, unable to move or speak. She had never been anyone's dinner guest. She knew how to serve, but she wasn't sure she knew how to sit.

"Now hurry," urged Miss Dover. "We have a lot to talk about before Gil gets here."

Damaris turned and left then, clutching her shawl tightly about her. As she slipped out of her plain dress and into the "special" one, a daring thought entered her mind. She would wear the brooch. Her mama's. If she was to be a dinner guest she wanted to look her very best. Perhaps the brooch on the bit of lace at her throat would give her confidence.

She withdrew the brooch from her drawer and held it up to the light, admiring again the sparkle of the stones. Then she reached for the watch and let it dangle from her hand as she grasped the chain. She still did not have the blue velvet or the domed glass. The watch must remain in its hiding place. She slipped it back into the drawer, covered it with her undergarments, and pushed the drawer quietly shut.

When she reappeared at the house across the street, dressed as bidden, Miss Dover exclaimed over and over how nice she looked. "The brooch is beautiful," she admired. "It must be a family treasure."

"Yes," said Damaris, lowering her eyes. "Yes, it is."

Then Damaris was seated in a chair in Miss Dover's own bedroom while the woman skillfully pinned her long, silky dark hair into a becoming style on top of her head. As Miss Dover worked, she talked, sharing with Damaris the fine art of table manners. It was not difficult for Damaris to listen. She realized that the pointers were given out of love and to keep her from embarrassment. Over and over in her mind she reviewed the "rules."

"If you get mixed up," said Miss Dover, "just watch me. I'll give you a little wink—or nod."

Damaris agreed. There were so many things to remember. She wondered if she could ever keep them all straight.

"Now—just before Gil comes I want to tell you a bit about him."

Damaris wondered why, but she held her tongue. Her head was so full of new information that it would be silly to ask for more.

"Gil came here when he was about thirteen," said Miss Dover, plunging right into her story. "Oh, my! That's fourteen years ago. How time passes!" Miss Dover was silent for a moment, seeming to think back; then she went on with her story. "He was skinny and scared and filled with mistrust—and I don't blame him one bit. He had lost his parents when he was only three and had been placed in an orphanage some place. He never has told me where. He doesn't like to talk about it and I try not to push. Well, he'd had enough by the time he was thirteen—and he ran away, somehow ending up out here. He looked like he hadn't eaten for days and his clothes were little more than rags. I fell in love with him the moment I saw him. You see—I had always wanted a boy of my own."

Miss Dover stopped. Damaris wondered if she would be able to continue, but she did not hesitate for long.

"Well, it took a lot of doing, believe me, but I finally earned his trust. We found him a job with a local rancher—a friend of mine, and Gil worked hard and saved every penny he earned, determined to have his own spread. And then Gil came up with a plan to share-crop the calves. He took those that would have died without special care—or something like that. I never could understand exactly how it worked, but both parties seemed more than satisfied with the arrangement.

"The man would gladly have let Gil work for him for the rest of his days. He was so pleased with Gil's care of the animals. In fact, I think he would have even left him the spread in his will. He hinted as much to me. But that wasn't what Gil wanted. He was determined to make his own way. So he got a small piece of land, put a few head of stock on it, mostly the calves he'd earned, which had grown and had calves of their own, and spent part of his winters cutting timber to sell in town. In short, after a few years and much hard work, he now has a paying spread. It's small, but it will grow. And Gil seems quite pleased with his accomplishments."

She gave the girl's hair one final pat. "I think of him as my boy. Oh, I never formally adopted him—just sort of 'accepted' him. But he's mine—nonetheless." She laughed softly, then added, "And anything else you wish to know—you'll have to get from Gil himself."

Damaris, though touched by the story, couldn't imagine why Miss Dover would expect her to show further interest.

Chapter Sixteen

Christmas Day

Damaris could not hide her nervousness as she sat at dinner with her hostess, Miss Dover, and Gil Lewis. Damaris had never shared a festive table with anyone before. She was so conscious of her table manners, or lack of them, that she feared she would break out into a sweat.

But Damaris was quick to learn. She had listened closely to all that Miss Dover had said. She watched her hostess carefully, every now and then receiving a smile of encouragement or a nod of approval. Even so, Damaris found it hard to relax and enjoy herself. She wasn't even able to take much part in the conversation. Miss Dover and Gil chatted comfortably. Damaris sensed that they had discussed many issues in the past, and today was simply a matter of catching up on the latest happenings in each other's lives.

They made attempts to bring Damaris into the conversation. When asked a direct question she gave an honest, though short, reply, but she never did relax enough to really become involved.

Nor did she wish to. Damaris held herself in check, giving no information about her experiences in the past, her feelings about the present, nor her thoughts and dreams about the future. Damaris was careful to reveal nothing about herself.

She felt relief when the leisurely meal was finally over. Now she could slip to the kitchen to clean up and let the other two chat by the comfort of the blazing fireplace.

But it wasn't to be so. After Gil's heartfelt declaration that the meal he had been looking forward to for weeks had been even better than he imagined, Miss Dover stood, smiled at them both, and then turned to Gil.

"Well, now it's time for you to pay your dues."

Damaris wondered what she meant and was surprised to see Gil remove his jacket and lay it aside. He followed this by carefully rolling up his sleeves, his face playfully screwed in mock displeasure.

Miss Dover chuckled softly, then turned to Damaris to explain.

"Gil always does the washing up at Christmas."

Damaris could not believe what she was hearing. She had never seen a man "wash up" in her entire life.

"But—but I will do it today," she stammered.

"Oh no," insisted Miss Dover, "we have had this arrangement for years."

"But—but I—I have—haven't been here before," replied Damaris.

"You may dry," conceded Miss Dover. "That is usually my chore—but this year—with the three of us—I'll care for the food and put the clean dishes away."

"But—but—I expected to do it all and I don't mind—really," Damaris hastily continued.

"Now, Miss Damaris," said Gil in his pleasant drawl, "if you wish to be a part of this little family, then you must accept your assigned task without argument or conditions—or else pay the consequences. I learned that long ago." He smiled at Miss Dover, then turned to wink at Damaris, causing her cheeks to flame.

Damaris was too flustered to argue further. She hurriedly turned to the table and began to gather dinner plates and cutlery.

The clean-up proceeded as planned, though the kitchen seemed crowded. The man bending over the steamy pan of hot water took up much more room than either woman. Damaris listened to the light chatter and easy laughter. He had spoken of her as part of the family. Damaris was so affected by the thought that she could hardly keep the tears from her eyes. In one way she longed to really be a part of what was going on around her. At the same time she held herself back. She dared not let her heart rule her head. One could be dreadfully hurt by becoming too involved.

"Is that it?" Gil asked as he glanced around the room.

"That's it," replied Miss Dover.

"You are definitely getting to be a smarter cook," he teased. "When I was a kid, you used to dirty three times the dishes—and just for the two of us."

Miss Dover laughed and her pleasure filled the small room with silvery merriment. "Oh, Gilwyn," she replied with good humor, "you were the one who made the 'rule' in the first place. You said it would be more fun to do things together on Christmas."

He nodded, sober now. "And I was right," he insisted, pouring the water from the dishpan into the big pail by the door and wiping the pan so he could place it on the wall hook. "Besides," he went on, "it has stood me in good stead as a bachelor. I never leave the dishes for more than three days at a time—while other fellas don't wash up for a week—or two."

Miss Dover laughed again, and Gil smiled when he saw the look of horror on Damaris's face.

"He's just teasing," Miss Dover defended. "I have been to his place—several times—and I have never seen dirty dishes stacked about yet."

Gil didn't pretend further. He rolled his sleeves back to proper position and buttoned the cuffs. "Are we going to play checkers?" he asked.

Miss Dover placed the last dish in her cupboard and turned to him, a slight frown creasing her smooth forehead. "I've been thinking about that," she replied. "Checkers is a two-person game, and now we are three."

Damaris realized that she was being considered part of the group, and the comment made her heart beat faster. She didn't wish to be locked in too tightly with this twosome.

Being a friend of Miss Dover's was one thing—but to be considered a part of a family that included a man—that was quite another.

"I—I don't play checkers," she announced. "You go right ahead. You two. I'll—I'll just watch."

Damaris wished she hadn't added the last statement. The truth was, she did not even wish to watch.

"Well, we'll play the first game then," said Miss Dover.

"We can make it a tournament," suggested Gil.

"But I don't play. Really," said Damaris again.

"We'll teach you then," said Gil as he went to a drawer to withdraw the board and the checkers while Miss Dover placed an extra chair at a small table.

"You sit right here and watch us," she said. "We'll explain the game as we go."

Damaris felt trapped. She sat in the chair as directed and carefully folded her skirts.

At first she held herself back, determined not to become involved in the game, or the players, but in spite of her resolve her interest grew. She was surprised at the intensity Miss Dover gave to the game. The two played skillfully, each intent on winning, but it was Miss Dover who eventually won the game.

"Great move," Gil conceded. "You got me on that one. I'll have to keep it in mind for next time."

"Now you play me," said Miss Dover to Damaris, apparently eager for another turn at the board.

"Oh, but I couldn't. I mean—this is the first time I've seen the game. I couldn't—"

"Gil will help you. We'll both coach you along."

Damaris could think of no polite way to argue further. She took the challenger's chair and Gil pulled his chair up beside her. It was unnerving to Damaris. She felt her hand tremble as she reached for the checker for her first move.

She was surprised at how much she had already picked up about the game. Gil often responded with a "Good," or "Right," as she made a move. When in doubt she would turn her eyes to his and look for his nod of approval or his whispered alternate move. Even Miss Dover gave approval or advice from her chair opposite. Damaris started to enjoy herself when she got into the game.

Damaris and Gil finally won the game. Damaris knew that Miss Dover had not played with the same intensity as she had during the game with Gil, but still her heart raced with the thrill of victory.

"Now I must play Miss Damaris and you coach," said Gil as he moved to exchange chairs with Miss Dover.

Damaris breathed a sigh of relief. It had been disconcerting to have him so close, whispering his bits of instructions into her ear. She was certain she would be able to relax and play a much better game with Miss Dover at her side.

But in the end, looking up into the earnest, intense blue eyes unnerved her every bit as much as his presence at her elbow. It was Gil who won the game, in spite of Miss Dover's good coaching.

"Oh my! Look at the time," Miss Dover exclaimed when the third game ended. "We must get some lunch before you have to take to the trail home."

Gil placed a hand on his stomach. "I'm still full from dinner," he protested, but he did not argue further when Miss Dover hustled toward her kitchen to put on the coffeepot.

Damaris rose quickly to follow. She had no intention of being left in a room alone with Gil and his unnerving blue eyes.

They fixed cold turkey sandwiches and a plate of cookies and tarts and took chairs close to the fire. Damaris was much more comfortable with this arrangement. The room was cozy and warm, even though the frost had completely covered the window.

They talked of simple things. Weather, neighbors, tasks that needed to be done. The fire crackled and snapped, spilling out its warmth. For one unguarded moment, Damaris wished she really could be a part of this family. Intense loneliness washed over her. It was not homesickness. She missed her mama in those moments when she would allow herself to think of her, but she was not homesick. She never wished to return home to her past circumstance.

As she listened half-heartedly to the chatter of her companions, Damaris let her thoughts wander. Memories came in rapidly, small scraps of disconnected pieces, yet they merged and intertwined to make a disturbing whole. Christmases past. They had not been times of pleasure for Damaris. Nor would they be for her mama this Christmas, Damaris mused.

It was even later back home. Her mama might even be in bed by now. She might be alone. Any excuse for a celebration sent her pa scurrying off to the town saloon to find comradeship and as much whiskey as he could afford. Poor as he was, he always found money for too much liquor.

Her mama would worry about his homecoming—hoping that it would be peaceful—and strangely—worry even more that he might not come home at all.

Damaris jerked her mind back to the present. She did not wish to think about home. It was much more pleasant here, in this room, with these two people.

She cast a nervous glance toward Gil. He was a man. Yet he had made no mention of whiskey in connection with Christmas. Nor had he visited the local saloon. Damaris wondered about that. Then she thought again of Captain Reilly and Mr. Brown. They hadn't used every excuse available to find a bottle, either.

Maybe there really are men who don't drink, she concluded. The idea startled her, though she'd had it before. She wondered how many sober men she would have to know before she could finally believe one, finally trust one. Recently she had started telling herself that not all men were like her father. But she always reverted back to the same old feelings—the same old fears—the same old conclusions. She stirred restlessly in her chair and brought two pairs of eyes to rest upon her. She flushed.

"Are you getting tired?" asked Miss Dover with concern. "I know you get up early. I'm afraid I'm a sleepyhead and sleep in until eight. I forget about those who must rise at six."

Damaris shook her head. She was not tired. She wondered if she would even be able to sleep when she did go to bed.

"I must go," Gil announced. "I hate to, but I must." He reached to set his cup on a nearby table. "This has been a wonderful day—but it is time now for the closing ceremony."

Miss Dover rose and went to get her Bible from a nearby shelf. Damaris felt her heartbeat quicken, as it invariably did at the sight of the book.

Miss Dover passed it over to Gil and he turned quickly to the page he sought. The story he read was of the first Christmas and the birth of the Christ Child. Damaris leaned forward as she drank in the words. They seemed so—so powerful, so full of wonder. She longed to believe them, to accept them as truth.

When Gil finished the account, he laid aside the Bible and closed his eyes. Damaris continued to stare as he spoke words of recognition and thanksgiving for the love that prompted the events of long ago. Suddenly realizing that he was praying, Damaris ducked her head and shut her eyes tightly. She had never heard anyone pray before. Something within her stirred at the sacredness of the moment. She felt as if she were walking across a newly scrubbed floor with dirty shoes. She squirmed, but even her discomfort could not keep her from straining to hear each word of the prayer.

Gil talked just as though he were speaking directly to God himself. Damaris had never heard anything like it in her entire life. You would have thought that Gil was best friends with the one to whom he was praying. And yet there was an earnestness, a hushed appreciation to his voice. Damaris could not understand it. This Gilwyn certainly was a strange individual. Peculiar. In her confusion, Damaris decided to give him a wide berth. She couldn't understand him at all. Although she had enjoyed this day as part of the family, she did not wish to have him try to foist his strange ways upon her. She longed for the prayer to end so she could breathe more easily again.

It was not a long prayer, and Damaris soon had her wish,

but even after the amen, the feeling of restlessness stayed with her.

Gil rose and placed the Bible carefully on the table.

"This has been good," he said, "but the trail home is a long one."

"I wish you could spend the night at the boardinghouse and take to the trail in the morning," Miss Dover said wistfully. "I just hate to think of you out in the cold—in the dark."

He brushed her cheek with his hand. "You worry too much, Mother," he chided gently. "I'll be fine."

It was the first time Damaris had heard him call her Mother. Mother—not even Ma or Mama. It sounded nice. He spoke the word so naturally, and yet with such deep feeling. Damaris felt her heart stir with emotion. She rose to her feet to make the feeling pass more quickly.

"I'll get your things," said Miss Dover and she moved to retrieve his heavy wraps.

He accepted the coat and shrugged into it. Then he reached for the leather gloves. Before pulling them on, his hand went to a pocket and came out with a small packet.

"For you," he said, passing the gift to Miss Dover and leaning over to kiss her cheek.

"Oh my!" she squealed, as excited as a child. Her cheeks flushed as she unwrapped the gift. "Combs," she bubbled. "New combs. Oh, I just love them. Look at them, Damaris. Aren't they beautiful!" She took his face in both of her hands and placed a kiss on his clean-shaven cheek. "Thank you, my dear. Thank you so much."

For a moment his hand rested on her hair as he looked deeply into her moist eyes; then he turned to Damaris.

"And this is for you," he said, reaching into his other pocket.

Damaris caught her breath. She had not expected any such thing. She had not even considered giving him a gift. She was unable to extend her hand to accept the package.

"But I—" she began.

"I didn't bring a gift my first Christmas here, either," he

said easily. "Mother has a way of making people feel at home—giving or receiving."

Damaris extended her hand. She still felt embarrassed, but terribly curious.

A length of lace tumbled from the small package that her hands nervously unwrapped. Damaris was too moved to speak.

"It will be perfect for that new dress you will make," enthused Miss Dover.

Damaris lifted her eyes and nodded her head. She could not find her voice, but she did manage to look up at him for just a minute. She saw understanding in the blue eyes before she quickly looked down again.

Confusion made her head whirl. A minute ago she had decided to stay out of his way. It had seemed so settled. And then he offered her a gift, a beautiful gift. If she accepted it, how could she then refuse to become a part of this—this strange yet beautiful family?

She wished he had not brought the gift for her. She wished she could hand it back. She wished they were not standing there looking at her. Accepting her. Welcoming her.

It was all so—so much. Damaris wasn't sure whether to smile or to weep. She had never felt so full of emotion. She didn't want to be feeling—feeling everything so deeply now. She wished to rush home to her little room, bury her head in her pillow, and shut out all the strange, disturbing thoughts and sensations that were washing through her.

As Damaris fought to gain control of herself, the man moved out into the coldness and darkness of the night. Damaris felt the chill wind as it swept into the room, sensed the movement of the older woman, heard her sighs of concern as she thought of his long ride home, then heard the door close sharply against the night.

Damaris finally brought herself under control. She was still holding the lace, letting its delicate pattern run through her fingers. She pictured it on the bodice of the dress she hoped to sew. It would be so beautiful. Her new dress might just match the becoming little bonnet in elegance, after all.

"I suppose you are anxious to get home, too," Miss Dover was saying.

"Yes. Yes, I must," Damaris responded, her voice sounding to herself as if it were somewhere off in the distance.

"Oh my," responded Miss Dover with such force that Damaris lifted her eyes in response, giving her total attention to the older woman.

"I almost forgot in all of the excitement of the day," she said hurriedly. "I found the verse."

Damaris looked puzzled.

"The verse," repeated Miss Dover. "The Bible verse about your name. I found it. I wrote it down right here. You can look it up when you get home."

Damaris felt her heart begin to pound. Miss Dover had found her name. Her Bible name. The name she had been searching for so long. Damaris wondered how she could have possibly forgotten to share it with her until now. She reached eagerly for the piece of paper and stared at the words. Acts 17:34. Acts 17:34. She couldn't wait to get home to read the passage. But it did seem strange that it was only one verse. The story of Daniel took several chapters. So did the accounts of Joseph, Noah, and Moses.

She must mean this is where it starts, reasoned Damaris as she tucked the small scrap of paper protectively in her dress pocket. Damaris knew that even if she should lose the bit of paper, she would not forget the reference. It had been burned into her mind. Acts 17:34. She would never forget it.

She thanked her hostess for a wonderful day, clutched her shawl tightly about her shoulders, and dashed out into the cold darkness and across the street to the boardinghouse.

She hoped there would be no one about when she entered the back door and slipped off to her room. She wanted no delay or disturbance as she settled herself in her room to read the verses she had for so long wanted to read. The story of the woman whose name she bore.

Chapter Seventeen

The Name

"He can't stay here tonight and that's final!" Mrs. Stacy shouted in anger.

Damaris closed the door as quietly as she could and held her breath so that no one would hear her enter.

A male voice that sounded like the sheriff's answered. She could not make out the words but the tone sounded as if they were meant to calm the distressed woman.

"I will bide no excuses," returned Mrs. Stacy in her loud voice, this time raised a pitch higher. "He was told before. He's ruined Christmas for all of us. I will not have it. Do you hear? I will not."

The sheriff spoke again. Damaris caught the last few words. " . . . in the jailhouse until he sobers . . . but it is unbearably cold there."

A shiver made its way through her body. Someone—someone in the boardinghouse had found a Christmas bottle. She moved forward another step wanting to escape to her room. Surely she would be safe there.

"I don't care about the cold. He brought it on himself. Perhaps the chill will bring him to his senses."

Damaris paused in her flight. Perhaps Mrs. Stacy needed her. Needed her to fend off the drunken attacks like she had always done for her mama. Damaris froze to the spot, anger and fear gripping her. She wished to run, to hide, but she could not move.

A new voice joined the din. Someone was moaning—or singing—Damaris wasn't sure which. "Oh, hush up!" Mrs. Stacy cut in harshly. "You'll waken everyone in the place."

Damaris wondered how Mrs. Stacy could think that anyone could be sleeping with the commotion that she herself was making.

"I can bed him down in my room on the floor," said the sheriff. "He'll pass out an' sleep until—"

Mrs. Stacy interrupted the sheriff. "Not with my bedding and on my carpet. I won't have him—"

"Very well," said the sheriff, his voice weary and filled with resignation. "I'll git one of the fellas to help me git him over to the jailhouse."

"And the sooner the better," insisted the woman. "Look what he's done. Just look. And Damaris still out celebrating. Maybe if she'd been here—"

"Thet wouldn't have made any difference and ya know it," the sheriff argued, his voice raised for the first time. "He was out to make a ruckus and he woulda done it no matter who was or wasn't here."

Damaris felt her stomach tighten. What had gone on in the dining room? Had she been wrong to take the day off? She took another silent step toward her bedroom but just as she moved, the door to the kitchen opened and Mrs. Stacy stepped through. Her hair was disheveled, her eyes swollen from tears, and her face dark with anger and frustration.

"Oh, there you are," she said as she jerked to a stop at the sight of the girl. "I was about to send someone over to get you. We've got a terrible mess in the dining room. That— that ol' fool of a miner—" But Mrs. Stacy got no further. She flung her apron over her face and burst into tears again.

Before Damaris could take another step the sheriff poked his head through the door.

"Mrs. Stacy could use a cup of good strong tea," he said to Damaris. "Her place has been pretty much torn apart."

Damaris managed to nod her head. She lifted the shawl from her shoulders and hung it on the hook by the door. Then she crossed to the stove to check on the kettle. It was still steaming, so she went for the teapot and the tea.

Her hand stole into her pocket and fingered her slip of paper. "Acts 17:34," she said to herself. "Acts 17:34."

While she prepared the tea she heard commotion in the dining room. More than one voice spoke as the sheriff and his helper manhandled the drunken miner and removed him from the premises. Damaris had no desire to enter the room until all the men had left.

"Here you are, Mrs. Stacy," said Damaris, passing the woman the cup of strong tea. Damaris wasn't sure if Mrs. Stacy heard; she was still crying loudly into her apron.

Damaris eyed Mrs. Stacy. She could detect no cuts or bruises, but Damaris knew that many painful injuries could be hidden.

At last Mrs. Stacy removed the apron from her face, dabbed her eyes, and sniffed away her remaining tears.

"He was even worse than last time," she fumed. "I told him then that he couldn't come again if . . . But he promised. Oh, he swore he was off the liquor. 'Turned over a new leaf,' he said. Humph!"

"Where are—are you—hurt?" asked Damaris. She had never even asked her mother such a question. Not in all of the years they had silently suffered together.

"Oh, he didn't touch me," the woman said quickly. "The sheriff was right there. But no one was quick enough to stop him from tipping the table and scattering my best china all over the floor."

She began to weep again and Damaris recoiled. The sympathy she felt a moment before suddenly evaporated. Why was the woman making such a fuss over broken china? Her mother had responded with less emotion to a broken arm.

"I'll clean up the china," said Damaris woodenly as she moved to the dining room.

It truly was a mess. Two tables had been tipped. Broken china was strewn across the room, and food had scattered and stained the rug. A tablecloth lay with its hem drinking from a pool of cranberry sauce. The drapery at the window was half pulled from its mooring and dangled haphazardly.

A plant of red geraniums had been uprooted from its pot, and dirt trailed across the floor to where the plant now lay, its roots bare and broken.

Damaris let a hand reach into her pocket again before she went for the brooms and mops to clean the mess. It would not be an easy chore and she knew that it would be some time before she would settle in her own room with her Bible propped up before her. If only she could have read the story before she'd had to take on this unwelcome task.

Without warning, anger started to burn within her. It was the whiskey. No, it was those who were foolish enough and selfish enough to drink the vile stuff. Selfishness—that's what it was. No consideration for anyone else, for how they felt, or for how they suffered. Pure selfishness. Such people didn't deserve love. They didn't even deserve to live. It would serve them right if they fell in their stupor and bashed in their stupid heads. Mrs. Stacy was right. Let the no-good miner freeze to death in jail. It would be no more than he deserved.

Never in all of her years of being the victim of her father's rages had Damaris felt such sudden and intense anger. It shocked her, but she did not repent. For an awful moment she wished she had stayed at home. Stayed and fought back. She was older now. Stronger. She was sure that she, with her mama, could put up quite a fight. They might not win, but they could inflict some damage before they were beaten. In that awful moment, Damaris longed for the chance, the opportunity to cause bruise for bruise, cut for cut, cruelty for cruelty.

And then, as quickly as it had come, the rage was gone, leaving Damaris trembling and troubled. Should she feel shame? Remorse? Damaris could not sort her troubled thoughts. She cleaned the mess as quickly as she could so she could retire to peace and quiet as soon as possible.

It was late when Damaris finished cleaning the room. Things were now in order. The broken dishes had been cleaned up and thrown into containers for disposal. The drapery had been rehung, though it still looked a bit disturbed after its ordeal. The carpet had been cleaned and rinsed, but not all of the stains would come out. The tables had been righted and covered with fresh tablecloths. The stained tablecloth was soaking in the kitchen in an effort to remove the cranberry stain. Damaris had done all that she could do. She sighed and blew out the light.

Mrs. Stacy had taken to bed hours before, begging a terrible headache. Damaris was no longer angry with the woman. She was no longer angry with anyone. She felt numb as she threw out the dirty water and hung up her mop.

"I'm still going to read it," she promised herself. "No matter what time I have to be up in the morning."

Damaris was about to go to her room when she remembered the doors. The sheriff had not returned. Mr. Starsky, the man who helped lug the drunken miner to the jailhouse, had come back to inform Damaris that the sheriff would be spending the night at the jail to keep the fire burning in the big iron stove. Surely he would not get much sleep on this cold night.

Damaris went to secure the bolt on the front door. Then she checked the door at the back. It was firmly locked. Damaris sighed again and glanced once more around the kitchen before heading for her bedroom.

As she set the lamp on her small stand, she reached up and slipped the bolt on her own door. She seldom bolted her door, but tonight she had been unnerved. The curse of whiskey had followed her all the way out West. Perhaps she would never feel safe again.

Damaris looked down. She was still wearing her best gown. In her confusion and anger she had forgotten to change it. She wanted to cry as she looked at it. It was so soiled and stained that Damaris wondered if she would ever be able to get it clean again.

She removed it carefully and slipped on her worn, secondhand robe. Then, lamp in hand, she went again to the kitchen and pressed the dress into the tub of water with the tablecloth. She did hope that the stains would not be permanent.

As she prepared for bed she heard the wind. It was blowing gustily now and the temperature would drop quickly. *I wonder if Gil has reached home safely?* she thought, glancing at the bedside clock. It was almost one o'clock. She nodded to herself. "He'll be in. Long ago," she mused with some satisfaction, surprised at the relief she felt.

Then she climbed into bed and pulled the covers up as far as she could and still be able to turn the pages of the Bible.

Acts 17:34, she reminded herself. She flipped through the book until she found Acts. She had lately been reading in the book of Acts herself.

"Just look," she murmured. "I would have discovered it for myself soon. I was almost to it."

With great anticipation she found chapter seventeen and ran her finger across the verses until she came to verse thirty-four.

What was the woman like whose name she bore? What mighty deeds of bravery or kindness had she done? Damaris could not wait to find out.

"Howbeit certain men clave unto him, and believed: among the which was Dionysius the Areopagate, and a woman named Damaris, and others with them."

Damaris let her eyes quickly pass down to chapter eighteen. Now she would read the whole story.

"After these things Paul departed from Athens, and came to Corinth; and found a certain Jew named Aquila, born in Pontus, lately come from Italy, with his wife Priscilla; (because that Claudius had commanded all Jews to depart from Rome:) and came unto them.

"And because he was of the same craft, he abode with them, and wrought: for by their occupation they were tentmakers."

Damaris was disappointed in the turn the story had taken. She read on and on, hoping to return again to the woman Damaris. But the more she read, the more it was apparent that the story of Damaris was sadly lacking. There was just no more there. Nothing about the woman. The next chapters and verses went on to speak of others and what they had done.

Damaris concluded that she must have missed something. She flipped back again to Acts 17:34 and reread the verse. She read it again and again. Finally her mind accepted what her brain had been trying to tell her. There was nothing more there about Damaris. No words, no mighty exploits, no acts of kindness or deeds of bravery. She had done nothing. Said nothing. She had just been. Damaris felt disappointment seep all through her body and soul.

With an angry thrust she pushed the Bible from her and heard it fall to the floor with a sickening thud. She did not even lean over to blow out her lamp. She pulled her blankets up about her ears, buried her face in her pillow, and let the tears flow.

Never had Damaris felt so completely defeated, so alone and miserable. Even the Bible had nothing to say about Damaris. She had been rejected by both heaven and earth.

Chapter Eighteen

The Truth

Damaris felt a heaviness as she climbed from her bed and dressed for her duties of the day, and not all of it was due to her lack of sleep.

She could not put into words the deep sorrow that settled over her after her discovery of the night before. There was nothing—nothing to the story of the Bible Damaris. No wonder Miss Dover had looked at her blankly when she mentioned that her name came from the Scripture. Nobody, not even one as faithful at reading her Bible as Miss Dover, could possibly have paid any attention to the one-line account.

Damaris felt her cheeks grow warm with shame. How would she ever be able to face the kind woman again? The woman who knew her secret. Damaris had thought her biblical name gave her worth; now she knew that the woman in the Bible also was of no account. Damaris left her room with a heavy heart and put her mind to the morning tasks.

Burying herself in her task had worked in the past, but it did not work well for Damaris on this difficult morning.

Mrs. Stacy appeared in the kitchen just as Damaris was ready to serve the few boarders who showed up for breakfast. The woman was still out-of-sorts and complained that her headache was no better. Damaris had just suggested that she take a pot of tea and retire to the dining room when the sheriff appeared. He was starving, he informed Damaris, and also needed some hot black coffee for the man at the jail.

Damaris quickly complied. She did not want to annoy the sheriff when he was in such a foul mood.

"Crazy man snored and moaned by turn all night long," the sheriff continued as Damaris poured his coffee and served him bacon and eggs at the kitchen table. "I was 'bout ready to take Mrs. Stacy's advice and let 'im freeze to death."

Damaris said nothing.

"Never got more'n a few winks sleep all night long," he continued, rubbing his hand over his unshaven face.

Damaris placed the toast on the table along with a small pot of jam and turned back to the tub of soaking items to find a job for her hands. She lifted the tablecloth. It still bore the stain of the cranberry juice.

"Thet from last night?" asked the sheriff.

Damaris was surprised that he was watching her.

She nodded her head and wrung out the tablecloth. If the stain had not been removed by now, more soaking would not help.

She placed the tablecloth in another pan and turned to her dress. Most of the stains and soil had soaked out of it, she found with relief. She lifted it in the air to let some of the water drain from the garment before she wrung it out.

"Thet yers?" asked the sheriff around his bite of bacon and eggs.

Damaris nodded again.

"Messed it pretty bad?" asked the sheriff.

"I—I plumb forgot I was wearing it," Damaris admitted, a flush touching her cheek. "When I came in and—and everything was in—in such a—a state, I just went to work."

The sheriff nodded, seeming to understand.

"Ya figgered out the damages?" he asked her.

Damaris's eyes widened with surprise. "No-o," she said, shaking her head.

"Well, you git thet fer me as soon as you can. I'll sober him up and send him on home. But iffen he's goin' to celebrate in such grand style—it's goin' to cost 'im. He don't have nothin' better to spend his gold pieces on. Figger the dishes, the carpet, the wasted food, the tablecloth there, yer dress—

and yer time, too. Itemize it all out and I'll give the list to 'im."

Damaris, though still surprised, nodded in agreement. How would she ever make such an estimate?

"You just write the things down," the sheriff went on. "Anything thet was broke—or damaged. I'll put the prices to it."

"I'll get right to it," Damaris agreed, "just as soon as I have finished serving the breakfasts."

Later in the morning the sheriff returned with the pail in which he carried his hot coffee—now holding several gold pieces. He passed a few to Mrs. Stacy, who promptly forgot her aching head. Then he turned to Damaris. "These are fer you," he said. "Fer your dress and your work."

Damaris looked at the coins. She had no idea how much they were worth, but she guessed they were of considerably more value than her simple gown and her time.

"But—" she began.

"Take 'em," said the sheriff, pressing them into her hand. "I coulda charged him twice the amount an' he woulda known it was fair. Ya jest can't run around breakin' up other people's property fer them to clean up after you."

Mrs. Stacy nodded vigorously in agreement, a smug look on her face. "You can't," she agreed. "That's a fact. I'm goin' to have to travel all the way to the city to replace those broken dishes and that damaged carpet. And the drapery needs to be replaced, too. And my tablecloths. Even my dress. It was all splattered."

It seemed to Damaris that Mrs. Stacy had compiled herself quite a lengthy list.

Damaris dropped her coins into her apron pocket. What would her mama think if she could see her with the money? Even though her thoughts turned to her mother, she would not let them rest there. No good could come of allowing herself to think of home.

Instead, Damaris thought of Mr. MacKenzie's store and

his yard goods. Perhaps she would be able to pick out some material that would be worthy of the delicate lace she had tucked away in a corner of her drawer. Damaris felt her cheeks redden and her breath quicken at the thought.

And then her thoughts went further. She would need to sew the dress on Miss Dover's machine. Damaris dreaded their next encounter. The woman was sure to ask her about Acts 17:34.

The next day she showed Mr. MacKenzie her gold pieces and asked him what she could afford with the coins. His eyebrows shot up and he whistled softly.

"Must have been some dress ya ruined!" he exclaimed.

Damaris felt a tinge of guilt. "But the dress isn't ruined," she hastened to explain. "Oh, it has a few small stains—but you can scarcely see them."

Mr. MacKenzie nodded. "Well, he still caused it damage, I guess, or the sheriff wouldn't have charged him for it."

"Some of the money is for my work," Damaris continued in her effort to explain.

"Had lots of cleanin' up to do?" asked the man. "Suppose it took ya most of the night."

Damaris flushed again. "I—I was done by one—actually," she admitted.

Mr. MacKenzie nodded again. "An' on Christmas, too," he said as though that made it much more costly.

Damaris was surprised to learn that her money would purchase the nicest piece of material in the store with a good amount still left on her account for future use. She held the beautiful fabric protectively as she left the store later in the day. As much as she dreaded the conversation that was sure to ensue with Miss Dover, Damaris could not resist slipping in to show her the fabric.

Miss Dover clucked and fussed over the material in fitting manner. Damaris had forgotten her anxiety when the woman suddenly turned the conversation to the dreaded subject.

"Did you get a chance to read Acts 17:34?" she asked, excitement still touching her voice.

Damaris did not look up. Her cheeks warmed as she nodded her head.

"Wasn't it exciting?" continued Miss Dover. "It made me wish that I could put my name in there. Just imagine, 'A woman named Katherine.' You must have been so excited."

Damaris still did not lift her eyes.

"Funny I never noticed it before," went on Miss Dover. "But if it had said Katherine, I'm sure I would have paid more attention."

Damaris looked up then. She still said nothing, but her troubled eyes looked directly into the dancing eyes of the older woman.

"What is it?" asked Miss Dover candidly. "You don't seem pleased."

"I—I guess—I guess I was—was disappointed," stammered Damaris, knowing that her words did little to convey her emotion.

"But why?" asked Miss Dover.

"Well, she—she didn't say anything. Didn't do anything," blurted Damaris, her eyes threatening to flood with tears. Damaris jerked herself stubbornly to attention. She refused to allow tears to spill.

"But she did!" said Miss Dover, her face showing shock at the words. "She did!"

Damaris looked confused. "What?" she asked blankly. "What?"

"Why, she did the most important thing anyone can ever do," went on Miss Dover. "Didn't you read it?"

"I—I read the verse. That's all I found. Just the one verse. Did you find more—someplace?"

"No," admitted Miss Dover. "I just found the one verse— but it contained so much."

"But she didn't do anything," insisted Damaris again. "It just went on to another story—of someone else."

"But it had already said all that needed to be said," argued Miss Dover. "Here, let me show you," and she hastened into the back rooms and came out with her Bible in hand.

Damaris felt relief wash over her. Miss Dover had more in her Bible than Damaris had in hers. It would soon be straightened out. She would be able to see for herself the whole story.

Miss Dover seated herself on the little bench and nodded Damaris to her side. Then she opened the book to the seventeenth chapter of Acts and began to read the familiar verse.

"Howbeit certain men clave unto him and believed: among the which was Dionysius the Areopagate, and a woman named Damaris, and others with them."

Miss Dover looked up from her reading and beamed at Damaris as though she should be pleased. Damaris was more confused than ever. Those were exactly the same words she had read for herself. There was nothing there about Damaris.

"But—" Damaris began, then let her words hang lifeless.

"Don't you see?" asked the woman beside her.

Damaris shook her head. The tears were hard to hold in check. "She didn't do anything," she repeated stubbornly.

"But she did! She believed! She believed! Oh, Damaris, that is the most exciting, the most important thing anyone can ever do. Then—and now."

It was Miss Dover who now let tears fall unheeded. "She believed. She believed," she repeated. "It's wonderful. Just wonderful."

"Believed what?" asked Damaris, puzzled.

"Why, the message Paul brought to Athens. About Jesus. About Him being the Son of God. The Savior. That we can be freed—forgiven—by trusting Him. You must go back. Read the chapter again and again until you understand it. Look! Here in verse three, 'Christ must needs have suffered, and risen again from the dead: and that this Jesus, whom I preach unto you, is Christ.' And here, in verse twenty-seven, 'That they should seek the Lord, if haply they might feel after him, and find him, though he be not far from every one of us: for in him we live, and move, and have our being.'

"Go back, Damaris. Go back and read it all slowly and carefully. Find out for yourself why it was so important that Damaris believed. I'll be praying for you as you read—that you might discover the truth for yourself."

Damaris nodded dumbly. She would go back and read— as many times as it took—until she could understand why Miss Dover was so excited about the fact that the Damaris of the Scriptures had believed the report of the man called Paul.

————

It took Damaris many days and many readings until she began to understand the meaning of the Scriptures. She had to go back and reread the Gospels again and again. At last she was able to put the stories of the life and death of Christ together with the persistent teaching of the Apostle Paul. "It is true," she whispered to herself as she lay tucked in her bed one night. "All the stories about Him are true. He really lived—and died—and lives again. And I can know Him. Can know Him—in my—my very being. In my heart. My mind. I don't really know the spot—but I know that He can be with me—in me—just as the Bible says."

That night, tucked under blankets to ward off the chill of the room, Damaris became a believer. Warmth more comforting than that of any quilt flooded her whole being as she took the important step of faith. She still did not fully understand it. She still had much to learn. She still had many troublesome scars from her past that needed healing, but she knew one thing with certainty. She was a believer. Just like the Damaris of the biblical account. She had made her own, deliberate, thoughtful decision, followed by genuine repentance and a prayer of faith.

She found it hard to sleep that night, so anxious was she to share her discovery with Miss Dover. She knew that the older woman would be thrilled to know that her prayers had been answered.

Chapter Nineteen

Scars

Damaris lived with the joy and peace of her newfound faith for two years before her past began to trouble her. Gradually she became aware of her intense feelings toward her father. She had tried to push them aside and not think of the anger that accompanied any thoughts about him. He was just some distressing presence from her past. She was through with him—finished. Why should he bother her now?

Yet as Damaris continued to read the Bible with greater understanding, she kept coming across disturbing passages that spoke of forgiveness—of love. She began to wonder if the Jesus she now served expected her to forgive one who had so often and so cruelly wronged her.

Try as she might, Damaris could not push aside the matter as easily as she once had. But neither could she forgive. She struggled with her problem but she did not discuss it. Not even with Miss Dover. Damaris pretended that the bitterness was no longer buried within her—and for the most part, she succeeded in hiding it from others.

She maintained her three part-time jobs. From the serving tables and the kitchen of Mrs. Stacy's boardinghouse, she would hasten across to Mr. MacKenzie's store to stock shelves or wait on customers. Then she would hurry off to Miss Dover's and sew as fast as she could treadle the machine until it was time again to help prepare the evening meal.

After her kitchen work was done, she would often scurry

off to Miss Dover's again to put in a bit of work on her own garments before climbing into her bed and turning to her Bible.

She had her own Bible now. Miss Dover had seen to that. Damaris had never had such a treasured possession and she could hardly believe her good fortune. She read before she went to the kitchen in the morning and again when she retired at night. She memorized verses that caught her attention and reviewed them silently as she worked on one task or another. Every day she learned and grew—but she did not release her bitterness. She simply tried to smother it with the positive lessons she was learning daily.

There were many days when things went well and Damaris could forget that she had ever felt angry, bitter, and alone. She had her God. She could talk to Him as a friend— just as Gil had done that first Christmas she had spent at Miss Dover's. She had her Bible. She could turn to its pages for strength and direction. She even had friends—Gil would say "family," but Damaris still found it difficult to consider herself part of the family even though Gil apparently did not.

Yet, life was good. Damaris enjoyed keeping her hands busy and seeing her small account and her wardrobe grow. She was making out quite well on her own. She did not let herself think of the far-away home where her mama might still be struggling with her drunken pa.

Another spring passed to summer and summer to fall. Damaris marked another birthday, but again she told no one of the special day. She smiled softly to herself as she thought of her circumstance. She was nineteen now. Well past the age that her mama had said a girl ought to be able to be on her own. Damaris felt that she had come of age.

Gradually she began to open up to the people of the community—though one would hardly have said that Damaris was friendly or out-going. Yet she was kind and thoughtful. Especially with children. She still thought often of the young Edgar. Mr. Brown had not been to the MacKenzie store for many months, and Damaris ached to know how the young boy was doing.

He's no longer a baby, she reminded herself. *He's a boy now—and he'd feel ashamed to trail around on a woman's skirts. He likely wouldn't even remember me,* she told herself one day as she thought about him. She was not prepared for the pain that the acknowledgment brought to her heart. Then in typical Damaris fashion, she pushed the ache aside and determined to forget the little boy from her past and go on with life.

One day as Damaris dusted and straightened shelves at Mr. MacKenzie's store, she heard a faint rustling behind her. When she turned she could see no one. She knelt to her task again.

Then she heard a soft, whispery voice speak timidly. "Ma'am? Ma'am? I need sumpin'."

Damaris rose and scanned the room before her, still seeing no one. Then she spotted her—a small girl, not yet big enough to see over the counter.

Damaris smiled.

The fright went out of the pair of blue-green eyes, but the little girl did not smile in return.

"Could I help you?" Damaris asked.

The small one reached up to dump some coins on the counter from a sticky, moist hand.

"Mama needs some salt and sugar," said the shy child.

Damaris looked at the dirty face and soiled dress.

She would be pretty if she were clean, she thought.

Damaris got the salt and sugar and handed them to the girl.

"How would you like a penny candy?" Damaris asked.

The little girl shook her head.

"You wouldn't like a candy?" asked Damaris in surprise.

"I got no money," responded the child.

"Well, I—I am allowed to treat my friends," responded Damaris. "You see I have an account here." She pulled her account sheet from the counter shelf in front of her. "You see," she said, showing the card to the little girl. "I just write the candy here on my account and it is all paid for."

Damaris wrote the item and amount on the sheet and

then lifted a penny candy from a jar.

The child shook her head again.

"Don't you like candy?"

"Pa says thet takin' things is—is sharity," responded the little one.

"Charity? Not—not if it is—is sharing by a friend," argued Damaris. She waited for a minute as the child seemed to contemplate the dilemma. "Do you understand sharing?" asked Damaris.

The little head nodded and the eyes grew wider and more intense. "That's a pro'lem," she sighed.

"What problem?" asked Damaris.

"Willim and Tootles would want some, too," she explained.

"Willim and Tootles?"

"She's not really Tootles," explained the little girl, and for the first time she allowed herself a little grin. "We jest call her thet fer fun."

"What is her name?" asked Damaris, happy to have found a subject that brought a smile to the sober little girl's face.

"It's Florence," said the child. "Florence Ann."

"That's a pretty name," said Damaris. "I like it. And what is your name?"

"My name is Abigail. Abigail Prudence—but Mama calls me Abbie."

"That's pretty too," said Damaris.

The child tilted her head slightly and looked at Damaris. "What's yer name?" she asked suddenly.

"It's—Damaris."

"Dam-a-ris. I never heard thet name afore."

"No. It's not common," agreed Damaris.

"But pretty," said Abbie, wanting to return the compliment.

"Yes. I like it," said Damaris. "It's taken from the Bible."

Damaris felt pleased with her name now that she herself had become a believer. She wished she could explain it all to the little girl. She wondered if the child had ever heard any of the Bible stories. If she even knew that such a thing as a

Bible existed. Or was she as ignorant as Damaris herself had been?

Damaris still held the penny candy. She extended it to the child again. "I will give you one for Willim and Tootles, too," she promised with a smile.

"I'd better not," the child said, backing up a step. "Pa might not like it."

Damaris did not argue further but let the candy drop back into the jar. She did not want to get the girl into trouble.

Abbie left then and Damaris watched her go.

Poor little tyke, she thought as the door closed behind the small figure in the faded dress. *Doesn't even dare accept a penny candy.*

Then a new idea came to Damaris. "What we need in this town is a—a teacher!" she said aloud. "There's no one here to teach Bible stories to the boys and girls. I—I wonder if their folks would let them attend if—if someone like—like Miss Dover—or—or me—were to start a Sunday morning class in place of a church service?"

The thought was so new—and so exciting—that Damaris wondered why she had not thought of it before.

"I'll talk to Miss Dover when I go to sew this afternoon," she determined.

The remaining hours at the store seemed endless. Damaris chafed as she did her work, wishing she could leave immediately to tell Miss Dover her idea.

———

Damaris approached the subject cautiously with Miss Dover. She wasn't sure if she was being presumptuous in thinking she could take on such a sacred task.

"You know how you—you and Gil are always saying that this town needs—needs a church and—and a preacher?" she began.

Miss Dover raised her eyes from the dress she was sewing for Mrs. MacKenzie and nodded, interest showing in her eyes.

"Well, what would you think if—if someone were to—to

start—well, sorta classes for children."

"Sunday school?"

Damaris looked surprised. "Is that what you call it?" she asked.

Miss Dover nodded her head. "Classes where children are taught from the Bible? Yes, it is called Sunday school, because they are usually held on Sunday morning—and they are lessons."

Damaris nodded. It was exactly what she had thought of even though she couldn't remember ever hearing of Sunday school.

"It would be wonderful. I have prayed and prayed that someone would do that very thing," said Miss Dover.

"Then—then, why don't we?' asked Damaris.

"We? You mean us?"

Damaris nodded, her eyes fixed on the woman's face. She watched the cheeks turn slightly red.

"Why, I—I just never thought of—of doing it myself," the woman sputtered.

"But why not?" asked Damaris.

"Well, I—I—" Miss Dover completed her unfinished sentence with a shrug of her shoulders and an embarrassed laugh. "Of course—why not? I don't know why it never came to me before. Here I have been praying for years—when I could have been busy answering my own prayers. What a—a complete dummy I have been."

"Then you will help me?" asked Damaris.

"Yes. Yes. I'd love to help you. Why, that's exactly what needs to be done—at least until we can get a church. Who knows—if we get folks interested, we might get that church, after all. It's a wonderful idea. Just wonderful. I can hardly wait to tell Gil."

Damaris's thoughts turned toward the young man who was so busy that he seldom made it to town. She hadn't seen him in months, though Miss Dover said he had called on her once or twice.

———

The next weeks were busy with preparations and invitations. When the day finally arrived for the first Sunday school class, six children showed up. It was exciting for Damaris and Miss Dover. But they hoped for an increase in number within a short time.

Damaris was disappointed that Abbie was not among those in attendance. Damaris had found out where the child lived and had paid a personal call on the household. A surly man had answered her knock and asked gruffly what she wanted. Damaris felt her knees tremble as she tried to answer.

"My kids got no need fer Sunday school," he growled at her. She could smell the liquor on his breath, and her heart ached for the man's helpless children. Damaris retreated as soon as she was able, fear gripping her heart.

So the Sunday school classes continued without the Rudding children, though Damaris still prayed that the day might soon come when they too would be able to join the group.

She did see Abbie on occasion when the child came to the store for flour or salt, and once she met her on the dusty street. They always smiled at each other, but Damaris did not dare voice the invitation she longed to extend.

———

Damaris was in the store folding yard goods to place on the shelf when the door opened and a young woman walked in, a child on her hip, a small girl clutching her skirt, and another little boy in tow.

"I need some flour—and some yeast," the woman said in a trembling voice.

Damaris went to get the requested items. As she returned to the counter the door opened again and Abbie came in. The little girl gave Damaris a shy smile.

"This is Willim and this is Tootles," she explained.

When Damaris realized that she was serving Abbie's family, her smile widened.

"So you are Abbie's mother?" she said. "Mrs. Rudding?

I'm happy to meet you. I'm Damaris Withers."

The young woman lowered her eyes and nodded her head in brief acknowledgement.

"Abbie is a wonderful little girl," went on Damaris. "So nice and polite."

She hoped the young mother would be pleased to hear of her child's good behavior, but the woman neither smiled nor looked up. She seemed extremely nervous and fidgety.

"Would you like me to put this in a sack for easier carrying?" Damaris asked.

The woman managed a nod.

Damaris placed the flour and yeast in a small brown bag and was passing it to the woman when a man burst through the door, slamming it back against the wall and making everything in proximity shudder in his presence. He seemed to be in a rage even before he entered. Damaris recognized him at once as Mr. Rudding.

He strode directly to the counter and jerked the brown bag away from the woman who had just accepted it. Without a word he threw it back across the counter at Damaris. "I suppose this is your doin'," he growled. "Talkin' her into spendin' my money on yer foolish notions."

Damaris could smell whiskey again. Before she could bring herself under control, her body began to tremble. The woman before her was cowering as though expecting to be struck. The little girl dodged behind her mother's skirts, and the little boy ducked behind a wooden barrel and whimpered in fright. But Abbie stood firm in her place, not fleeing or fighting but prepared to take the brunt of the assault.

The scene was all too familiar to Damaris. She had been that crouching child when she had been younger. Then she had been like Abbie. Silent, unmoving, and prepared for the worst.

Damaris trembled for only a moment. Then the seething anger gave her boldness. She pushed herself to her full height, ready to give the man a piece of her mind or a piece of her fist, if need be; but the terrified look in the woman's eyes stopped her short. It would not do to challenge him. It would only bring more pain to his family. Damaris turned aside, her shoulders sagging. She was defeated again. It seemed there was nothing that could be done in the fight against alcohol. She turned her back and let the anger drain slowly from her, robbing her of strength and dignity as it left her.

She could hear the man pick up the coins from the counter, could sense the mother gathering her children and ushering them from the store. She heard the curses and the slamming door, and then everything was quiet again.

Damaris slumped against the counter, weak from the drain of emotions. She knew then that her old hatred, her old anger, had not been removed, only buried deeper within her being.

Damaris covered her face with her hands and let the tears flow as the sobs shook her whole body.

Chapter Twenty

Fires of Rage

Damaris was busy sewing at the treadle machine and Miss Dover was sitting on the cushioned chair to her right, hand-hemming a new baby dress, when the door opened and Gil entered. Miss Dover was immediately on her feet, her hands laying aside the garment and reaching out to the young man.

"Gil! It's about time. I thought you had forgotten all about me—about us."

Gil smiled and reached for the outstretched hands. "You know better," he teased and leaned to kiss the woman's forehead. Then he lifted his head, let his eyes rest a moment on Damaris, and smiled his greeting. "Hello, Damaris." He had long since ceased calling her Miss Damaris. Apparently he was determined to make her feel part of the family.

She answered with a smile of her own. She was beginning to feel comfortable with Gil. He never pushed, never intruded, never challenged her private thoughts.

"How are things at the ranch?" asked Miss Dover.

"Fine. Just got back from my first—my very first cattle drive. Took forty head of stock over to the freight yards. They brought a good price."

"Now you can fix up your house a bit," said Miss Dover enthusiastically.

Gil laughed and shook his head. "I've already spent the money," he chuckled, "and not on curtains and carpets. It went for some better stock—and winter supplies."

"Oh, Gil," said Miss Dover with such obvious disappointment that both Gil and Damaris laughed.

Then Miss Dover shrugged and winked at Damaris as she spoke to Gil. "You need a wife," she said. "She'd fix things up in a hurry."

"A wife?" said Gil. "Now, who would ever want to take on a task like that?"

Damaris turned back to her machine and began to treadle as quickly as her feet could move, her full attention given to the material that slipped smoothly under the needle.

"Come on in. I'll fix us some coffee and we can catch up a bit. Damaris, you need a break as well. Come on out to the kitchen."

Gil hesitated. "Actually, I just came from Mr. MacKenzie's store. He's heard that there is a woman in town in great need. I—I bought a few things and I—I wondered if you—or Damaris would come with me to deliver them. I—don't suppose it would look too good if I went calling alone. Particularly when I don't know her. She might—might not understand that I am just trying to help her and her little ones."

At the mention of "little ones" Damaris lifted her head again.

"Oh my," Miss Dover said sadly. "Are they really in trouble and we haven't even known? What a shame. Who is it, Gil?"

"Family by the name of Rudding. The man left some time ago and hasn't come back."

Damaris let out the breath she had been holding. A feeling of relief swept through her. Mr. Rudding was gone. Now the poor woman and her children would be free of his menacing presence. Now people like Gil and Mr. MacKenzie and she, Damaris, could do something for the family.

Before she could think about her actions she stood swiftly. "I'll go with you," she offered. "I know the family." Then, realizing what she had done, she shrank back. "I—I mean if you wish. If—If Miss Dover doesn't want to—to—"

Miss Dover waved a hand to bring Damaris forward again. "Take your shawl, dear. The wind is cool," she cautioned.

Gil reached for the shawl that hung on the peg by the door and draped it over Damaris's shoulders. Then he held the door for her and spoke again to Miss Dover.

"We won't be long. Then I'd sure love a little visit and that hot cup of coffee before I head for home."

Gil had a buckboard at the hitching rail just down the street, and he helped Damaris up and over the wheel and onto the high seat.

"So you know the family?" he asked as soon as they were settled.

"A little," answered Damaris. "The little girl, Abbie, has been to the store a few times. The mother was there once with the other children."

"How many does she have?" asked Gil.

"Four. And Abbie is the oldest. About five or six years old, I would think."

Gil shook his head. "That's quite a houseful."

Damaris nodded, thinking of the little girl with the big blue-green eyes.

"It's a shame about the father—" began Gil.

"No!" said Damaris quickly. "No, it isn't. It's—"

She felt Gil's glance swing to her and her face flushed. She had spoken too forcefully, too quickly.

"You know him?" asked Gil.

Damaris bit her tongue so she wouldn't spill out more of her feelings. "I've seen him a few times," she said slowly.

"And you didn't care much for what you saw," stated Gil in the form of an observation rather than a question.

"No," said Damaris, shaking her head. "No, I did not care for what I saw."

"And what did you see?" Gil probed, this time in a direct question.

"I—I called on the home when Miss Dover and I started our Sunday school. He—he was very angry. Said his children didn't need any—any part of it. He—he had been drinking.

I could smell it. Then Mrs. Rudding came to the store one day. Wanted a few groceries. Just—just flour—and yeast. She had the coins, but he followed. Tore the bag away from her and hurled it back on the counter and—and accused me of causing her to spend his money foolishly. He had been drinking then, too."

Damaris shivered. She pulled her shawl more closely about herself, pretending that the tremor came from the cold winter weather rather than from her frightening childhood memories.

"You're cold," observed Gil. "Here, take my jacket."

"No. No, I'm fine. Really. It—it isn't the wind. It's—"

But how could she explain her past and its effect on her to him? She didn't even understand it herself, and she could never talk about it to anyone else. No one would understand the fear, the torture of suspense, the anger that burned deep within, the stripping of self-worth, the feeling of being totally at the mercy of another. She shivered again.

"If you won't take my coat, sit closer," insisted Gil. "Let me shield you from the wind."

Damaris felt her cheeks glow with embarrassment as Gil turned her slightly so that she would be protected from the wind by his larger frame. She wanted to escape, but she held herself rigidly in place and soon had to acknowledge that he was right. It was much warmer up closer to him where the wind no longer could flutter her light shawl.

They soon arrived at the simple shack on the edge of town and Gil helped Damaris down.

"Perhaps it would be good if you'd go knock on the door," said Gil. "She will recognize you. I'll come along later with some of these groceries."

Damaris nodded and walked to the door, side-stepping clutter on the path as she went.

As she reached the door she saw some movement at the window. A small hand swept away a torn, faded curtain and Damaris saw Abbie's face, pale and thin, appear behind the dirty, broken glass.

Damaris knocked, but there was no response. She turned

back to the window and noticed that the girl was still staring out at her. She motioned to the door, asking her to open it, but the child shook her head. Damaris stood for a moment, uncertain, and then her hand went to the latch and she pushed against the door. To her relief, it opened. Damaris pushed it farther on its whining hinges and then entered the run-down dwelling.

"Mama said I wasn't to let anyone in," explained Abbie, but she looked relieved to have Damaris there.

"Where is your mama?" asked Damaris.

"She's in bed. Sick," answered the girl.

Damaris heard a scuffling noise in the corner and turned her eyes to see young Willim sitting on the floor. His thumb was in his mouth and tears had washed streaks down his dirty face.

"He's hungry," explained Abbie, "but we don't got no food."

"Where's Tootles?" asked Damaris.

"She's in bed with Mama. Mama's sleeping but Tootles won't come out. She just lays there and cries."

Fear gripped Damaris's heart. Never had she imagined that things would be so bad.

"Do you have wood for a fire?" she asked.

The child shook her head.

Damaris spun on her heel and went back outside, her eyes filled with horror, her face pale. Gil took one look at her and stepped quickly to her assistance, placing his hands on her shoulders to hold her steady.

"It's even worse than I thought," she explained. "The mother is sick in bed and the children haven't eaten in days. Could you find some wood for a fire?"

"Are you going to be all right?" Gil asked her, still not releasing her shoulders.

Damaris nodded stubbornly. She would be all right. She had to be.

Gil gave her shoulders a slight squeeze and turned back to the wagon. Without further comment he hoisted out a large box of provisions and carried it into the house, kicking aside debris from the path as he walked. Then he returned to the wagon, lifted an axe from the box, and strode off toward the clutter of bush that crept in close to the rear of the house.

Damaris was already in action. She first grabbed the water bucket that stood beside the door and headed for the pump in the yard. She was relieved when it worked without priming. Soon a stream of water was gushing into the pail.

"At least *it's* clean," observed Damaris.

Gil soon returned with an armful of wood. While Damaris cleared away scattered dirty dishes, he started a fire. Damaris heated water in a pot and a large pan, the only kettles she could find in the house.

The children said nothing. Just watched the hurried proceedings with large eyes.

Damaris's thoughts scrambled as she tried to decide what would be the fastest and most nourishing meal.

"There are some crackers in there," Gil whispered.

Damaris glanced toward the children. "We don't want to fill them up on crackers," she answered.

"No, but they need something—fast."

Damaris agreed and dug through the groceries for a handful of crackers. The children accepted them hungrily and Damaris had to turn her head to hide her grief.

"How's the mother?" whispered Gil, concern edging his voice.

"I haven't made it to the bedroom yet—maybe I haven't dared to look," responded Damaris, her eyes showing her fears.

Gil nodded and headed for the room at the back of the house.

Damaris heard a child cry. She supposed that little Tootles had reacted to a stranger. Then all was silent. Damaris waited for a few minutes—until she couldn't stand it any longer.

When she entered the room she found Gil cradling the little girl in his arms, gently rocking her back and forth. It took several minutes before Damaris could see anything else in the darkened room, but then she made out two forms on the bed. They both lay very quietly, the woman with the baby tucked in the crook of her arm. Damaris's heart quickened.

"We need a doctor," whispered Gil.

"But—" Damaris was about to remind him that the town had no doctor.

"I know," went on Gil. "The nearest one is over thirty miles away."

"Maybe I can feed her some broth," said Damaris.

"Broth? I don't think—Do you have broth?" asked Gil, his voice low.

"No," answered Damaris, "but I'm sure Mrs. Stacy does. She always keeps broth of some kind in her pantry, for soups."

"I'll go get it," said Gil. He passed Tootles to Damaris. The child began to whimper again, and Damaris hushed her and rocked her gently.

She left the dark room with its awful smell. She could stand it no longer. The two older children still crouched in the kitchen devouring crackers. Damaris reached for a handful for Tootles.

Damaris's eyes filled with tears. She had thought she'd had a hard life—but never, never anything like this. And to think that these little ones, this mother, were sick and slowly starving just minutes away from a town full of people.

Damaris could not believe how quickly Gil made the trip to Mrs. Stacy's and back. When he returned he not only had a kettle of broth, but the town sheriff as well.

The big man pushed his way past Damaris and headed directly for the dark bedroom at the back of the house. He was there for several minutes while Damaris busied herself with warming the broth on the now hot stove.

When he returned to the kitchen his face was pale. He shook his head sadly and glanced at the three children huddled together on the kitchen floor.

"It doesn't look good," he said in a hoarse whisper.

"How bad?" asked Gil.

Damaris could not speak.

"She's still breathing—but just."

"The broth will soon be hot," said Gil.

Damaris turned to stir the broth again so it wouldn't get too hot. She didn't want to burn the woman's mouth.

"The baby's gone," said the hoarse voice.

Damaris jerked her head upright, not wanting to believe the words.

"Are you sure?" she asked, horror gripping her.

"I'm sure," said the sheriff. "He's already stiff and—"

A strange cry escaped from Damaris's throat. She whirled from the stove and fled from the house. The tears flooding her eyes made it impossible for her to see where she was going. She tripped and righted herself, tripped again, and struggled on. She did not know where she was going and she did not care. Panting and weeping she pushed on, pressing deeper and deeper into the thicket behind the house. At last her feet tangled helplessly in fallen branches and she fell heavily to the ground. She lay where she had fallen, her whole body shaking with convulsive sobs. She did not even try to control her weeping. Anger, dreadful anger encompassed her. A hatred like flaming fire burned within her. The man Rudding and her father were all intertwined in her mind, and what bound them together was the strong smell of whiskey.

Chapter Twenty-one

Changes

Damaris felt hands on her shoulders gently lift her, and then someone wrapped something warm around her. She hadn't realized how cold she was until she felt the warmth.

"Damaris, are you all right? You are chilled through. I'm getting you to Mother."

Damaris tried to protest, but her chattering teeth wouldn't allow her to say anything. She needed to get back to the children. She had no idea how long she'd been out in the cold.

But she could not resist when Gil lifted her in his arms and started back through the tangled brush toward the house and the waiting wagon. He deposited her gently on a fur robe on the floor of the wagon box.

"The—the babies—" she finally managed to utter.

"They will have help soon. Lots of help. People are coming from town. The sheriff went to get them. The family will be moved to various households for care," Gil assured her.

Damaris felt relief. She closed her eyes and ached to go to sleep.

The bumpy wagon ride did not take long and before Damaris could move to leave the wagon, Gil was down from his seat, beside her, lifting her down, and carrying her again. Damaris was still shivering. Her whole body quivered with cold.

"Bring her in here—to my bed," Damaris heard Miss

Dover order Gil. She wanted to protest again. Miss Dover had only one bed. She did not wish to take it from her.

But Gil did as Miss Dover instructed him. He lowered Damaris to the warmth of the bed and then left the room, closing the door as he went. Miss Dover stayed behind and slipped off Damaris's high-top shoes and tucked the blankets up around her trembling chin.

"I'll be back in just a minute," she said softly. "You try to rest."

Gil returned almost as soon as Miss Dover had left. "Mother is getting some tea," he informed Damaris. He took her hand and began to rub it between both of his, coaxing warmth and life back into it.

"Tell me—" began Damaris.

"You must rest," said Gil.

"Tell me—about the family," insisted Damaris.

Gil held back no longer. "Mrs. Rudding and little Tootles have been taken to the MacKenzie's. They are nursing them there. Willim—it's really William—is at the Taylors'."

"Abbie?" asked Damaris faintly.

"Abbie is over at the Jaspers'."

"All alone?"

"Well—she is with the Jasper family. They have three near-grown girls."

"But she's all alone?"

"I—I guess so. No family—of her own—with her."

The arrangement disturbed Damaris, but there was little she could do. Silence hung heavily in the room for some minutes before Damaris spoke again. "The baby?"

"They—they are having a—a service tomorrow. The sheriff is looking after the details."

"Does—does the—the mother know—yet?"

"No," said Gil.

A tremor passed through Damaris, and Gil put a hand on her shoulder.

"They are trying to locate the father," he said.

Damaris shuddered again.

There was another heavy silence. Then Gil leaned toward Damaris.

"There's more to this, isn't there?" he asked.

Her face paled and she refused to open her eyes to look at him.

He waited a few minutes and then spoke again.

"Do you want to talk about it?"

Damaris started to shake her head and then changed her mind. Her face wrinkled up as though she were going to cry again, but she bit her lip to gain control and gulped once or twice to calm herself.

Gil stroked the hair back from her face.

"It's the—the drink," choked Damaris. "I—I know what it's like. I know. I've—I've lived through that—that terror. My—my pa—"

Damaris could say no more. She turned away from the gentle hand that stroked her head and buried her face in her pillow.

"I'm sorry. I'm sorry." Gil tried to comfort her. "I didn't know. I—I shouldn't have made you talk. We won't talk of it again—unless you want to."

She did not cry for long. By the time Miss Dover entered the room with the tea tray, Damaris had blown her nose and wiped her eyes.

———

Damaris was determined to be up and about the next day. The whole town seemed to be abuzz with news of the family's peril that had developed right on their doorstep. Everywhere Damaris went she heard more stories—some of them dreadfully exaggerated accounts.

She tried to close her ears to each new version. The truth was bad enough.

The baby boy was placed in a small wooden coffin and buried in the cemetery on the hill overlooking the town. Most of the town folks were there to take part in the simple ceremony performed by the sheriff. Whether concern or curiosity brought them was a matter of opinion.

The woman still clung to life, but tenuously. Mrs. MacKenzie shook her head sadly when she greeted Damaris at the store. On the third day a message came by wire from a neighboring town to the sheriff. A man bearing the description of Sam Rudding had been killed in a brawl a couple weeks earlier. It seemed that the children were without a father.

Damaris felt no regret when she learned of the man's death, but then her conscience began to upbraid her.

"He is lost and *doomed* to hell," a voice said.

"And I can't think of anyone who deserves it more," her own bitter voice answered.

"Is that a Christian attitude? Would Jesus have responded in such a manner?" asked the first voice.

Damaris did not answer. Though she knew what the answer would be.

That night when Damaris knelt beside her bed to pray, her soul was heavy.

"God, I need help," she whispered, tears coursing down her cheeks. "I can't carry this load anymore. I can't. Bitterness weighs down my soul. It will destroy me if—if something isn't done. But I can't let go. I can't. I've tried. I can't let go."

Damaris cried into her pillow again, but her heavy burden was not made lighter.

Gil brought the sad news to Damaris and Miss Dover. Mrs. Rudding had passed away.

"What's going to happen to the children?" Damaris asked quietly.

Gil shifted his weight, his face drawn. "They are to have a hearing sometime next week to decide," he answered.

Miss Dover daubed at her eyes with a lace hankie and then blew delicately. "Poor little souls," she said with deep compassion.

Damaris reached for her shawl. "Do you mind?" she asked Miss Dover, her hand trembling. "I think I need a little walk."

"Go ahead, dear," responded the woman with an understanding nod.

Damaris did not allow her eyes to lift to Gil's. She passed him as quickly as she could. She wasn't sure where she was going but she needed to get out. To think. She walked the length of the town street with brisk steps. Something had to be done but she had no notion of what it was. Into her mind came the face of little Abbie, eyes big with pain and grief. And then there was William, skinny and under-sized for lack of nourishing food. And little Tootles, still confused and whining for her mama.

Life seemed so unfair. Damaris might have gone under with the cruelness of it all had she not had two years of walking and talking with her Lord. Even now, she was deeply troubled.

"What's the meaning of it all, God?" she asked, her face lifting to the sky. "Why is the world so heartless? So painful?"

Damaris was surprised when she looked up to find herself a few yards from the broken-down shack that had belonged to the Rudding family. She hesitated, not wanting to go near, and then moved forward slowly, as though compelled.

So much clutter. So much—mess. Mess. That was it. The whole place was a mess—inside and out. Just like the lives of the people who had lived there.

Damaris lifted her skirts so as not to drag them through the debris and found a large rock at the back of the property. She sat down and studied the scene before her. She still could not think. Could only pray in broken, disconnected thoughts and sentences. On her heart was one thought. *What will happen to the children?*

Their mother, father, and baby brother were all gone. What deep and painful scars would be left on their young lives?

Damaris prayed and cried by turn, but she got no closer to a solution.

"May I?" asked a male voice behind her.

Startled, Damaris jumped.

"Sorry," apologized Gil.

"That's all right. You just caught me off guard," she explained.

Gil moved forward and took a seat on the ground beside her. He said nothing. Just let his eyes gaze over the wreck of a house before them.

"I wonder who lived here," said Damaris after several minutes of silence.

Gil turned quickly to look at her. His eyes asked the question he was afraid to put into words: Had all the distress caused her to block the Rudding family from her mind?

Reading the question on his face, Damaris explained, "I— I mean—before. Before the Rudding family moved in. They haven't been here that long, you know. And nobody seems to know where they came from."

Gil nodded. "Well, I remember a widow living here. She had about ten kids—or so it seemed. And a big garden. The place looked much different then. Neat and trim with a little picket fence out front. And chickens. I remember chickens. Some of those fancy little ones that strut around and make all the fuss."

"Bantams?"

"Bantams. That's it."

Damaris laughed in spite of her heavy thoughts.

"Ten kids?" she asked next. "Where did she put them all?"

"Well, it seemed like ten. Actually there might have been only three—or four," answered Gil truthfully.

Damaris laughed again.

Her eyes drifted over the wreck of a house and yard. "Was it kind of cute then?" she asked wistfully.

Gil studied her face for a moment. "I guess so," he answered. "I never really gave it much thought. But it was neat. Boy, those little rascals had to work."

Damaris smiled—but laughter did not come. When she spoke again she surprised herself with her daring question. Really she had no right to ask for the information.

"Miss Dover said you grew up in an orphanage. What was it like?"

Gil's eyes darkened for a moment; then he turned to her and answered candidly, "Not nice. We each had our own little bed, our own shelf area for our one change of clothes, our own dish at the table, our own second-hand pair of shoes."

He paused.

"But that wasn't the hard part," he went on. "The hard part was not having anyone on your side. All of the kids stood alone, like we were afraid to stick together. Each individual against the entire force of—of disciplinarians." He paused longer this time.

Damaris was busy with her own thoughts. Then Gil went on. The words seemed hard for him. "I—I've always wondered—in the back of my mind—if I have brothers or sisters—somewhere."

Damaris looked at him and saw the pain in his eyes and the working of his jaw. He picked up a small stone and tossed it at an old tin pot lying half-buried several feet away. Then he went on. "They called it a 'home.' But it wasn't. Not in any sense. The rules were rigid. The discipline tough. We were not even allowed to cry."

Damaris shuddered. She didn't even want to think about it.

"So I ran away," he said frankly. "Just as soon as I found the opportunity."

There was silence again until Gil picked up a twig of wood and snapped it between his fingers.

"I ran away, too," said Damaris.

Gil did not even look up. He broke another piece of the twig and nodded in understanding.

"But it wasn't from an orphanage. It was from a—a home. And I wasn't alone. Not really. I had my—my mama. We sorta—stood together—though we never talked of it. Never."

Gil nodded again and waited for her to go on.

"Looking back now I realize—I realize that Mama sorta told me to go. Oh, not in so many words, but she put the idea in my head. I—I think she wanted me to get away from it. I don't think she wanted me—wanted me locked into what she had endured for all those years."

"Have you heard from her?" asked Gil.

"No," said Damaris sadly. "I haven't even dared to write for fear it would make more trouble for her with Pa."

"The whiskey?"

Damaris nodded, her eyes misting.

They sat quietly for a few more minutes and then Damaris broke the silence.

"Are you bitter?"

Gil's head came up and he looked directly into the deep brown eyes. "Bitter? Why?" he asked frankly.

"Well—about life? About your circumstances? I mean—you had nothing to do with your folks dying. Just like I had nothing to do with my pa drinking."

Gil waited to answer. Then he spoke softly. "Guess I was. Once. Before I met Miss Dover. Then after—after she finally broke through the barrier I had put up, and taught me from her Bible, well, after I had accepted God's Word as truth and asked for forgiveness for my own wrongdoing, then I was slowly able to forgive others too."

"I can't," admitted Damaris. "I still can't. I've tried—but I just can't."

"I don't suppose we ever can—on our own. Only God can work that miracle."

"But how? How do you let go?"

"I suppose each person has to work it out in his own way," said Gil slowly. "For me—it was—well, the realization that all things happen for good. Oh, not the orphanage really, or the drink, either. That wasn't part of God's plan. But even the bad in life has a purpose, I think."

"A purpose? What good can possibly come from—from so—so much bad?"

"I'm not sure how to—how to say it. But thinking of it like that—it helped me get over my hurt. I—well, I said to myself—that if I accepted my past—put it to use in my life—then it wouldn't be wasted. I mean—it seems to me that painful experiences can be used to better prepare us for heaven. You see, if we let it, even pain can shape us—make us better people—get rid of some of the ugly parts of our humanity."

"It only strengthened my ugliness," confessed Damaris.

"But it doesn't need to," insisted Gil. "It can make us stronger, more compassionate, more understanding—more like Jesus—if we allow it to. And the more clutter we get rid of in our life here—the more we will be able to enjoy heaven—when we get there. So, pain can have a purpose."

Damaris still looked puzzled.

"Well, I know I don't explain it well—but—say—say two people are going on a journey. One prepares. He buys the right clothing for the climate. He reads all he can to learn about the area. He studies about the people. Learns the language. He gets himself prepared the best he can. The other fella—he just goes. They both get there—to the same place. But which one do you think will enjoy it the most?"

"I s'pose the one who prepared," admitted Damaris.

"Exactly. I think that is why—why God allows hard things in life. To prepare us. To knock off rough edges—pride, bias, envy, selfishness—so that when we get to heaven we will be more in tune—more able to enjoy the beautiful things we'll find there. Maybe that's what the rewards will be. A deeper appreciation of what we are given—what we are a part of. Do you understand what I am muddling through?"

Damaris nodded her head slowly. "I—I think so," she answered.

"Well, I don't know if it makes any sense to anyone else—but for me—well, it gives a special purpose—a meaning for suffering. If we take it right—let it shape us and cleanse us—then we are better prepared to enjoy the glories of heaven."

Damaris sat silently, thinking on his words. She had not allowed suffering to do any refining in her life. She was still filled with bitterness and anger. If she didn't give it up to God, the whole thing would defeat her. She didn't want that. She wanted to turn it around. To make it produce something of worth in her life.

"You're right," she said at last, a tear coursing down her cheek. "Do you—do you mind if I spend some time alone?"

Gil stood. "Of course not," he whispered.

"I just need to do some praying," Damaris said.

Gil reached a finger to wipe the tear from her cheek. "Mother and I will be praying too," he told her, and then he was gone.

———

Damaris did not spend long in her prayer time. It did not take long. She was weary of her heavy burden of bitterness. She wanted to make her past, with its pain and disappointments, into a stepping-stone for growth in her life.

"Take it, Lord," she prayed. "Please, take it from me. Cleanse my heart and help me to forgive. Might I be able to use my experience to be more understanding, more compassionate, more loving. Might it make me a better person so that—so that I might appreciate heaven more when I arrive. Make me more like you, Lord Jesus."

After a time of unrestrained tears and earnest prayer, the terrible burden lifted.

"Mama—I love you," Damaris whispered softly, even though she knew she was all alone. "I—I wish that I would have told you so. I—I hope you know."

And then Damaris had a new thought. She never stopped to reason it through before, but her heart swelled with the knowledge of it now. Her Mama loved her. Yet her mother had never spoken of it either.

"That's why. That's why you—you gently urged me to go. You loved me. You didn't want me to be the victim anymore. You—you decided to take it all—yourself."

Damaris leaned her head into her hands and cried harder.

"If—if only Pa didn't—" began Damaris, then stopped abruptly. "I—I guess he was a victim, too," she said aloud. "I had never thought of that. Never wondered what made him who he is. Never even thought to ask him what kind of home he grew up in. I wonder if—if his pa beat him. I wonder when drink got such a hold on him."

Damaris ran a shaky hand through her heavy hair that had come unpinned.

"Oh, God," she prayed silently, "help me to love Pa. Help me to—to somehow forgive the terrible things he's done. Help me to pray for him—like I pray for Mama."

After a few more moments in tears, Damaris wiped her eyes on the hem of her dress and reached to pin her unruly hair into some sense of control.

"I must write Mama," she reasoned. "She'll be wondering if I am all right. I must tell her—and Pa—that I'm fine. I must send her my love."

Damaris rose from the place where she sat and brushed her skirts.

"I'm a mess," she observed, one hand stealing to her hastily pinned hair as her eyes dropped to survey her wrinkled dress—and then she smiled. "But I'm in better shape on the inside than I have ever been."

She lifted her eyes to the clear sky above her and drew in a deep, contented breath, "Thank you, Father."

Then Damaris started for home, anxious to find pen and paper so that the letter to her folks could be quickly posted.

Chapter Twenty-two

The Children

She had seen Abbie only once since the death of the girl's mother. Mrs. Jasper had come to the store and had brought the little girl with her. Abbie was clean. Even her hair had been washed and braided. But the hand-me-down dress she wore was way too big and the shoes on her little feet slopped with each step. She looked pale and troubled and ran to Damaris as soon as they entered the building.

Damaris held her close, not trusting herself to speak.

"She's such a solemn little thing," said Mrs. Jasper in front of the child. "Never laughs or plays—only sits and looks woebegone."

Damaris rose. She wondered how Mrs. Jasper could expect anything else from the child.

"Well, the hearin' is tomorra—and then I'll be done with it," the woman went on. "We got no room in our house for another. Maude had to share her bed—and didn't think much of it, either."

Damaris still said nothing but felt a mixture of excitement and sadness. Abbie was not wanted by the Jaspers.

———

The problem of the children was spoken of freely by the town folk. Everyone who entered the store seemed to have a solution.

"I wouldn't mind takin' thet littlest one," one woman observed. "But the boy—he don't look healthy. Don't know what one would ever make of him."

"Thet littlest one," someone else said, "she's a real little whiner. Can't stand a child who whines all the time. I'd rather have the boy. He might be skinny—but he keeps quiet."

"Thet oldest—she's kinda pretty—but by the time they get thet age they usually have picked up all the bad habits of the home."

"Poor souls. Poor little souls," another woman said, the tears running freely down her cheeks. "Just wish we had more room."

Damaris wished to shut out all of the comments but she could not. Her heart became heavier and heavier as the day went on.

"Well, tomorra it will all be decided. Maybe they'll have to load 'em up and take 'em all to the city," said one unfeeling man. "There's nothin' of worth at the house to pay a fella fer their keep."

Damaris walked home from the store with a heavy heart, but by bedtime she had made up her mind. *I'm going to ask for Abbie,* she pledged.

"I'm going to ask for Abbie," she repeated as she prepared for bed. "I don't know how I will manage, but I'll find some way—with God's help I will find some way."

As Damaris knelt by her bed to seek God's will in the matter, she could not block out the skinny face of little William, or the troubled eyes of tiny Tootles. "Oh, God," she prayed, "may someone want them, too."

She climbed into bed and began her reading of the Bible.

"I would have to pick that," she said in annoyance as her eyes fell on the words of Jesus: "Suffer the little children to come unto me, and forbid them not, for of such is the kingdom of heaven."

"That might be so, Lord," whispered Damaris, "but we are still on the earth. It seems that not many folks feel that way in our little town."

As Damaris closed her eyes to sleep, she still saw the

words before her. "Suffer the little children to come. . . ."

———

The day of the hearing dawned cold and bright. Winter was approaching and everyone could feel the sharpness in the air. It was another reminder that each one would be hard put to care for the needs of his own family members.

"If it were spring—with the promise of crops and gardens—people might feel more generous," allowed Damaris as she walked the short distance to the sheriff's office where the hearing was to be held. "With winter—no one knows how difficult it might be to make it through. No one wants to take chances."

Damaris was surprised as she opened the door and stepped into the room. Already the place was crowded with people. Perhaps there were more interested in taking the children than she had expected.

The three little ones were at the front of the room, clinging together on a little wooden bench. All three faces were pale. All eyes large with fright. William looked even paler and skinnier than ever, and Tootles cried until trickles from her eyes and nose streamed down her face together. Small Abbie held them both, a look of defiance on her baby face, as though she would challenge anyone who tried to take them from her.

They were a pitiful sight and Damaris had to fight hard to keep the tears from her own eyes.

The sheriff rose to his full height and cleared his throat. He looked dreadfully uncomfortable in his role. He refused to even look in the direction of the children.

"Ya all know the sad circumstances thet bring us here today," he said. He rubbed his neck self-consciously before he was able to go on.

"We gotta somehow find these three little ones a place afore winter sets in—an' the way it's feelin' this mornin' we might not have long."

Damaris felt her stomach twisting. She had wanted Abbie—had been willing to sacrifice for the little girl—but as she looked at the three all huddled together on the bench, she knew she had been wrong. They could not be separated. They could not.

"Now, I don't know jest where to start. Maybe with the youngest one. Anyone here have a mind to take the little one?"

Damaris held her breath. "Oh, God," she prayed. "Show me what to do. Show me."

And then to her surprise she was raising her hand.

The sheriff looked at her in shock.

"You wantin' her, miss?" he asked in disbelief.

"I—I want them all—sir—please," said a hoarse voice that Damaris hardly recognized as her own.

"You—but—but you don't have a—a h—"

Damaris was sure the sheriff had been going to say "husband" but he changed it to "home."

"I—I know," responded Damaris in a faltering voice, "but I thought the children might—might like to stay in their own home."

"Their own home?"

"Yes, the—the house on the edge of town."

"But it's nothin' more'n a shack," spoke up someone.

"I—I know," agreed Damaris, becoming bold in her fight. "But it was sturdy once. It can be—can be fixed up. Cleaned. I've been in it. I know it can be made—made quite—comfortable."

The sheriff lowered his eyes and cleared his throat again. He seemed terribly uncomfortable with the situation.

"An' how about—about carin' fer 'em?" he asked.

Damaris knew he had to ask the question for the children's sake.

"I—I have some money. A little." Her cheeks flushed. She didn't have much. Then a new thought came to her. "I can sew—at home. There is far more sewing than Miss Dover can keep up to. And I can sew."

Damaris saw someone in front nod in agreement. She took courage.

"If we make it through this first winter—and we will—

then next year we can have a garden—and maybe some chickens—we'll manage just fine."

Sheriff Gordon fidgeted. Damaris knew he expected the proceedings to be difficult, but not this difficult.

"Miss—I admire yer—yer unselfishness in wantin' to take in three little ones—but I am also responsible to see to their well-bein'. As much as I know yer good intent—knowin' you like I do—I still don't think it possible fer a mere girl to be able to provide fer three little ones on her sewin'. Iffen ya had some help now I'd not—"

"I'll help," offered a familiar voice from the back of the room. "I agree with her. They mustn't be separated. I'll help."

Damaris wanted to run to Gil and express her thanks, but the crowd held her where she was. She could not even see his face.

"In what way?" the sheriff was asking.

"I'll see to it that the repairs on the house are done, supply her with plenty of winter wood, and make sure they don't want for provisions," promised Gil.

Damaris knew that it was no idle, or easy, promise.

A murmur ran through the crowd. Everyone was talking at once. The sheriff lifted his hand for silence, and gradually order settled over the crowd again.

"Was there anyone who came here today with a mind to ask fer one of these children?" the sheriff asked in a voice that boomed out in the tight quarters.

No one responded.

The sheriff waited a moment, his eyes scanning the crowd.

"Then is there anyone who objects to Miss Damaris Withers takin' on the three of 'em?" he asked.

Again no one responded.

"Then I have a few more words," said the sheriff. "This tragedy has belonged to all of us. Iffen these two are willin' to take on the sole responsibility fer these little ones—then I think we oughta all be askin' ourselves how we can lighten the burden. A hand here an' there an' a full stew pot now an' then would be in order."

Then the sheriff turned to Damaris. "They're yours Miss Withers—an' God help ya."

Damaris waited no longer. She sprang forward and scooped all three little ones into her arms. Then she buried her head against them and let her tears mingle with theirs. The enormity of the task ahead hit her fully, and she feared that she would never be able to fulfill it. But suddenly peace filled her whole being. She wouldn't have to do it—not alone. She was sure that God had directed her to take all three of them. She had not even been prepared with arguments to uphold her claim on one. And yet she had them—all three— and even a house in which to raise them.

With the thought of the house, Damaris winced. There was so much to be done if she was to have it ready by winter.

"Come," she said. "Let's go home."

She lifted herself just as the last of the crowd left the room and there stood Gil, looking at her and her babies, a pleased yet concerned look on his face.

"We did it," she said, not really understanding her own words. "We got them."

He smiled and nodded his head; then his face sobered. "What do we do now?" he asked.

Damaris was taken aback. "Well, I—I guess we take them home."

"What about you?"

"Well—I—I need to go with them."

"And Mrs. Stacy?"

"Oh my," said Damaris. "I forgot about Mrs. Stacy. Well, I'll just have to go tell her that I won't be working for her anymore—and—and get my things."

"I'll get the buckboard," said Gil.

———

It was not an easy task to take leave of Mrs. Stacy. She had become far too dependent on Damaris. In fact, there were many household duties she had almost forgotten how to do.

"What will I do?" she moaned over and over. "What will

I ever do? I have boarders, you know. There's so much work with boarders."

Damaris nodded. "I am so sorry!" she exclaimed. "I would have given notice but I—I had no idea that—that it would turn out this way."

"Well, can't you at least work—part time?" pleaded the woman.

Damaris thought about it. "I can give you part time for two weeks," she said, "in exchange for room and board for me and the children."

Even as she spoke the words, Damaris wasn't sure how she would accomplish the task. But it would give them a bit of time to get organized—to fix up the run-down shack.

Mrs. Stacy looked hesitant, but at length nodded her agreement. She wasn't sure how well things would run with three young children underfoot.

———

The plan worked even better than Damaris had dared to hope. Abbie cared for the children while Damaris worked. They were fed in the kitchen and allowed to sit and play in the warmth of the big room while Damaris scurried about getting the meals ready or washing up the dishes. The in-between time was spent over at the little house trying to put things in order.

Mrs. Stacy was so impressed with the arrangement that she brought forth another proposal. "Why don't you just stay on here? It's working very well. There's no need for you to move off to that horrible little shack."

But the horrible little shack was daily becoming more livable. Gil was there mending the roof, fixing the broken windows, and supervising a good clean-up job. Along with him worked the sheriff and any other residents he could shame into taking a part. Bedding, clothes, and food contributions had also been forthcoming. Though Damaris found it hard to accept them, she vowed not to let her own pride get in the way of the children's comfort and well-being.

By the time she had completed her two weeks of work for

Mrs. Stacy, the little house was ready for them to move into and a nice stack of winter wood was piled neatly near the door.

Damaris packed up her belongings, bade the boarders and Mrs. Stacy goodbye, and bundled the children up as best she could against the cold winter wind.

"Come," she said to them. "We are going home."

Chapter Twenty-three

Home

Damaris was unprepared for the feelings that swept through her when she walked into the small house at the edge of town with three little ones in tow. The sole responsibility for their care and happiness rested on her shoulders.

She stopped and looked around her. The men had done a good job with the repairs, and Damaris herself, with the help of some of the women, had scrubbed and scoured until the place was at least clean—if not pretty. The three children looked around with wide eyes.

"It's—nice," spoke Abbie in quiet surprise. But William hung back, his hand clutching a handful of Abbie's skirt.

It was little Tootles who broke the spell. She suddenly broke into a grin and ran for the bedroom. Damaris followed, thinking the little one was out to explore. But when Tootles reached the room, she slid to a stop. The familiar bed was missing. In its place was a cot for Damaris and small beds for the children.

Tootles looked around, her eyes wide. "Mama?" she said softly, and then she began to cry.

Damaris took her into her arms and rocked her gently back and forth as her own tears joined those of the little girl.

"Oh, baby," she sobbed against the child. "I never thought. You thought you'd find her, didn't you? You poor little thing. How long—how long will it be until you forget?"

Damaris wasn't sure she would be able to endure the

grieving of the little ones. "Perhaps this was not a good idea," she said to Gil as he unloaded the wagon. "The reminders will bring pain instead of comfort."

"Give them a while," responded Gil. "They have as good a chance of adjusting here as anywhere."

Damaris busied herself putting things away as Gil brought them in. When she returned to the kitchen to make the evening meal, she found a fire already burning in the stove and a good supply of wood piled in the rough entry.

"Who's hungry?" asked Damaris.

"Me," answered Abbie.

"What should we fix?" continued Damaris.

"Pancakes," responded Abbie.

"Do you like pancakes?"

"Yeah. So does Willim and Tootles."

Damaris fixed pancakes, and judging by the volume the little ones ate, she had to agree with Abbie's assessment. It appeared that William and Tootles did like pancakes.

Damaris decided then that they would eat pancakes only on special occasions. They needed more nourishing food. Stews and soups and egg custards. Damaris looked at the thin little bodies and vowed to herself to have them filled out come spring.

After the children had been tucked in bed for the night, Damaris busied herself about the small kitchen-living quarters, trying to find ways to make the little house more "homey."

"I really haven't much to work with," she mumbled to herself, feeling a bit discouraged at the barrenness.

She hung a calendar from the store. The smiling face of the child with a puppy in his arms helped to brighten one wall.

"I think they will like that," she observed as she stepped back and surveyed her work, her head tilted slightly.

"If I could just—" she began, then quickly cheered. "I know. I will get a box of crayons or some simple paints and let the children make their own pictures."

Damaris felt much better. They would make a home. After all, it was people dwelling together and how they felt about one another that really mattered. For a moment Damaris thought of her own home, and an ache became heavy in her chest.

"I miss Mama," she said in a half-whisper. "I do hope—I pray she is—is all right."

The parting gifts given to her by her mother came to mind, and Damaris brushed a tear away as she headed for the small carpet bag that still held her treasures.

"Mama said that the watch should be displayed under one of those glass cases. Well, I still don't have the glass—or the blue velvet—but I guess she won't mind if I just hang the chain from a nail. And I'll pin the brooch on a pretty scrap of Miss Dover's left-over material and put it right beside it. It will make a nice bright spot on another wall—and be a reminder of Mama. I'll—I'll tell the little ones all about her—and the fine gifts that she gave me—tomorrow. She'll be—she'll be their—sorta "grandmother" even though they have never met her. I think they'll like that—having a grandmother."

Damaris lifted out the watch and the brooch, intent on carrying out her plan. Her fingers caressed the treasures as the tears coursed slowly down her cheeks. She drew the gifts of love against the softness of her cheek for a moment, then rose quickly to carry out her plan.

In spite of the help she received from others, it was a hard winter for Damaris.

The children were sick often because of their run-down condition. Damaris especially feared for William. It seemed that he always had a cold. Damaris coaxed and pleaded and tempted him with special treats to get him to eat. Still, he put on little weight.

Tootles began to gain. She seemed to soon forget her mother and before long was a laughing, teasing, mischievous child. Damaris adored her, even though she found her terribly hard to keep up to.

Abbie still had a special place in Damaris's heart. Damaris marveled at the girl's big blue-green eyes and brushed the silky hair until it shone. She allowed the child to sit beside her and sew while she worked at alterations from the stack of hand-me-down clothing that had come from the town folk. By the time winter moved in to stay, she had them all pretty well clothed, but her meager account at Mr. Mac-Kenzie's store was sadly depleted. She knew she would have to turn her time and attention to trying to earn some money.

She did take in sewing and mending, but she no longer had the use of Miss Dover's machine, so it was slow work and paid her very little.

"I'm going to have to figure out something," she murmured to herself one evening as she sat sewing after the children had been tucked into bed. "Maybe Gil—" No, she couldn't ask Gil to do any more than he was already doing. She knew that helping the family was costing him dearly from funds he had set aside for more stock.

"I don't know how I'd ever manage without the help of friends," she admitted.

Miss Dover often sent over little treats for the children in the form of cookies or puddings. Mr. MacKenzie was good about adding this and that to her grocery boxes when she shopped at the store. And Sheriff Gordon was often handing her change he said came from someone who was interested in her welfare. They were getting by. God was faithful in supplying as the needs arose.

———

"I really miss you," said Miss Dover as she sat at Damaris's kitchen table one afternoon drinking tea from the best cup Damaris could produce.

"I miss you, too," admitted Damaris, but as she looked about the room she knew she would not change what she had done.

"Is William feeling better?"

"He's not coughing as much—but his constant cold still worries me," admitted Damaris.

"It's too bad you couldn't get hold of some cod liver oil. It's supposed to be good for building up one's strength."

Damaris nodded. She knew of no place to purchase cod liver oil.

"I'd like you to come for Christmas," continued Miss Dover. "It shouldn't hurt him, should it?"

"I don't suppose so," said Damaris slowly, "if we wrap him up well. Though I don't know if I can carry both him and Tootles."

"Gil will come for you with the team."

Damaris nodded. Gil had been a frequent and welcomed visitor since she had settled in with the children.

"Can I bring anything?" asked Damaris. "I mean it's not like you are inviting one person anymore."

Miss Dover smiled. "The truth is," she said frankly, "I can hardly wait. I've never had children for Christmas before."

"And you may well never want to have them again," laughed Damaris. "They can be a little rowdy at times. Especially Tootles."

"Tootles," laughed Miss Dover. "That is such a silly little name. What did you say her real name is?"

"Florence," replied Damaris.

"Florence. That really doesn't suit her, does it? She's such a little bit of a thing."

"I thought we should continue to call her Tootles at least until the children have made some of their other difficult adjustments," explained Damaris.

Miss Dover nodded in understanding.

"They have had a hard lot, haven't they?" she said simply. "But they do seem to be settling in quite well. You make a good mama, Damaris."

Neither woman saw a little head lift and a small brow pucker in deep thought, but after Miss Dover left and Damaris had returned to her stitching, she felt a small body press up against her side. It was Abbie.

"Are you really our mama?" she asked, catching Damaris totally off guard.

"Well—I—I am the one who is caring for you," she stammered.

"But are you our mama?" persisted the little girl.

Damaris didn't know what to say. She laid aside the garment she held in her hands and drew the little girl close.

"What—what do you think? Would you—would you like me to be your mama—or would you rather I—I just stayed Damaris?" she asked.

"My mama," said the child without hesitation.

"Then—then we will—will think of me as your mama," said Damaris.

"Can I call you Mama?" asked Abbie.

Damaris was touched by the child's request, but she wondered what the town folk would say.

"Would it—would it make you feel—better—to call me Mama?"

The girl nodded again.

"Then—then I would like that," said Damaris, laying aside all concern about the town people. The child's needs were more important.

"I'd like it, too," said Abbie and her face broke into a grin.

With Abbie calling Damaris "Mama," it didn't take long for William and Tootles to follow suit. By the time the little family was picked up by Gil for the Christmas celebration at Miss Dover's, all three children were at ease calling Damaris by the name. Damaris had not yet become used to the title, but she had to admit that it did make them feel more like family.

Christmas was a good day. Like Miss Dover, Damaris had never shared a Christmas with children before. She was amazed at how much fun they added to the celebration.

Abbie was full of compliments for the hostess, though some of them didn't come off quite as she had intended.

"I like this," she said of the mashed turnips. "It tastes just like good food."

And again of the chocolate pie. "It looks kinda like mud

but it tastes lots better, doesn't it, Willim?"

Tootles only spilled her drink once and William kept most of his dinner on his spoon as he searched for his mouth. All in all, Damaris was quite proud of her little brood.

Following the dinner, gifts were exchanged. Damaris had spent late nights sewing rag dolls for Abbie and Tootles and a stuffed ball for William. All three squealed at their gifts, making the effort well worthwhile.

Gil also produced gifts. A little cup and saucer for Abbie. A spinning top for William, and a stuffed dog called Ruff for Tootles.

Then Miss Dover brought out gifts for the children. She had a slate for Abbie, saying that she would soon need to learn her letters, building blocks for William, and a cloth book with hand-stitched pictures for Tootles.

"Oh my," said Damaris with a pleased chuckle, "they will have so many new things to play with."

Besides the toys, Miss Dover had sewn each child a new outfit from her leftover material. Damaris was as excited about the clothes as the children.

Then the adults exchanged their simple gifts and Damaris left the children to play under the supervision of Miss Dover while she joined Gil in the kitchen to wash the dinner dishes.

"How are things going?" he asked when they were alone.

"Good," she replied honestly. "Oh, there are some bad days—and bad nights. Especially with William, but for the most part, things are going fine."

"I notice he is still coughing," went on Gil.

"I'm waiting for spring," said Damaris. "I pray that with the warm weather and sunshine he will get over it."

"Does he still waken and cry at night for his mother?"

"Not recently. He seems to be slowly adjusting."

"It's been hard for you, hasn't it?" Gil asked directly.

Damaris nodded. She could not deny it. But things were gradually getting better for all of them.

———

With the coming of spring and the return to sunshine, Damaris moved her little family outside as much as she could. They busied themselves planting a garden. Mrs. Boyle gave them a hen with nine chicks and they built a little pen and took great pleasure in watching the chicks grow. They cleaned the yard of its clutter and trimmed the bushes by the door, raked the path, and picked up the tangled branches at the back of the house for fire wood.

Damaris longed to paint the house, but she knew they could never afford it. She managed to be content keeping the window glass shining and the curtains inside fresh and clean.

As Damaris had hoped, William's health began to improve. He lost his hacking cough and his constantly runny nose and even began to put on some weight. Damaris was pleased to see his cheeks fill out and his little arms and legs begin to lose their scrawny appearance.

Baby Tootles began to say more words. Daily, it seemed, she added to her vocabulary, making the older children hoot and giggle with her attempts at mimicking.

"Isn't she funny," laughed Abbie. "She says 'ink' for drink an' 'popo' for porridge."

William laughed at his little sister, too, and Tootles just sat and grinned merrily, happy to be the center of attention.

"How would you and the kids like to visit the ranch?" asked Gil one day when he stopped to see how they were doing.

Damaris could not even be heard above the din that went up from Abbie and William. Even Tootles joined in, sure that something exciting must be taking place to make her older siblings holler so.

"Well," chuckled Gil, "I guess that settles it."

Damaris nodded. She had never been to Gil's ranch. Had never really expected to, but the outing would be good for the children. In fact, she admitted when she was able to give it a bit of thought, it would be nice to drive out in the countryside for a change.

"When would you like to go?" asked Gil.

"Why, I don't know. Any nice day," responded Damaris.

"Let's go today. Let's go today," called Abbie. William began to call after her, "Today. Today." Then Tootles took up the serenade, "Day. Day," she called loudly, her eyes glistening with the fun of it all.

"Sh-h," quieted Damaris. She could scarcely think, let alone talk. The clamor settled down and Damaris ventured an answer. "I guess we shouldn't wait too long," she replied, "or I will get no peace and quiet."

Gil grinned. "I'll try to arrange it so that I can stay over next Sunday after our Sunday school classes and we'll go bright and early Monday morning," he promised.

Damaris nodded her agreement and Abbie could not resist one more cheer.

Chapter Twenty-four

Family

The family sat together on the high seat of the buckboard. Tootles sat on Damaris's lap, tucked securely within the arc of her arms. Gil held William, who clutched the end of the reins, pretending he had control of the team. Abbie sat between them, one hand extended each way, resting gently on the adults who framed her.

The day was bright and sunny and the whole mood was one of celebration.

"I've never been on a visit before," said Abbie, bouncing with anticipation.

Damaris looked down and smiled. It was good for the children to get away from their own yard. It was good for her also. She had not been beyond the confines of the town since arriving there with the wagons from the east.

With that thought came memories of home. They were no longer painful to Damaris. She could think of her mama without the awful battles of guilt and of her father without the bitterness becoming strong in her mouth.

"Did I tell you I had a letter from my mama?" she asked Gil.

His eyes focused on her face.

"They are fine," Damaris went on quickly, reading the interest and concern in his deep blue eyes. "I—I wrote to them after—after I finally made peace with—with my past."

There was a moment's silence before Damaris went on.

"I really didn't know what to say. I mean, I couldn't truthfully say I was sorry I had left. I couldn't even say 'I forgive you' because—well, because that would be saying that they were—wrong. So, I just shared with them my—my experience of reading the Bible and understanding that I could have forgiveness for—for my past—everything. And about the—the peace I have felt since. Then I told them I loved them and hoped they were getting along fine."

Gil nodded.

"It made me feel better," went on Damaris, surprised that she was sharing so much of herself with the man beside her. It did feel good to let it spill out, though.

"And she answered you," said Gil.

Damaris knew he understood how much the letter had meant to her. "I'm going to write them again," said Damaris, "and tell them about the children."

Her eyes circled the three little ones who accompanied them, and love glowed there.

Gil did not miss it.

"Look," shouted Abbie, breaking into the conversation, "a eagle!"

Damaris and Gil both laughed. "It's not an eagle, honey. It's a crow," said Damaris. "Perhaps we'll find you an eagle before we get to the ranch."

Abbie's young eyes took in everything along the way, but William kept his eyes on the team, content to sit and yell occasional instructions to the horses. They hadn't gone far at all when Tootles fell asleep.

"I thought that might happen," said Gil, "so I threw in a few blankets. You can make a bed for her here at our feet."

Gil stopped the team while he arranged the blankets, and Damaris laid the child down. Already her arms and back had begun to ache from the weight of the little body. She flexed them to take out the kinks. The ride resumed with Damaris and Abbie playing their own little game of "I spy."

The sun rose higher in the sky. William's eyelids drooped, but he refused to give up his grip on the reins and join Tootles on the bed on the floor.

"It's a long, long way to the ranch," Abbie observed.

Gil chuckled. "We are almost there," he told her. "It's right over that next hill."

Even Damaris was pleased to hear the news.

As they topped the last hill, Damaris saw a neat yard with a barn and corrals off to the left and a trim little unpainted house tucked against a stand of trees on the right.

"Oh, Gil," she said before she could stop her tongue. "It's perfect."

Gil looked more than pleased. He looked elated.

"You like it? Well, I will admit that it suits a bachelor fine, but a woman might see a good number of things that she'd want fixed up—just like Mother says."

Damaris let her eyes travel from the outdoor pump to the small vegetable garden to the hammock stretched lazily between two trees. A smile lighted her eyes. Right in that little spot between the barn and the garden would be a great place for a chicken pen, she was thinking. Then she blushed at the thought.

"What's all them things in that big pen?" asked William.

"You mean, you haven't seen cows before?" asked Gil.

William shook his head.

"Yes, he has," cut in Abbie, nodding her head vigorously and making her braids bounce back and forth. "He just forgetted."

"Those are some new ones I just bought," explained Gil. "I'm keeping them there for a few days before turning them out on the range."

"They look nice," observed Damaris.

Gil beamed. "They are good stock," he admitted. "They should help build up my herd."

The team wanted to travel right past the house and on to the barn but Gil reined them in. "I'll help you get these little ones inside," he said, "and then the first order of business should be something to eat."

"Yeah," said Abbie, clapping her hands together. "I'm hungry."

Damaris and Gil both laughed. Gil helped Damaris and

Abbie down and then passed the sleeping Tootles to Damaris. "Lay her on my bed," he instructed softly.

Abbie was already scurrying about the yard exploring everything at hand. William still clutched the reins, determined to be in the wagon for as long as it moved. "I'll take this one with me," said Gil as he swung up onto the high seat again.

Damaris was surprised when she entered the house. It was bigger than it looked from the outside. In fact, it contained four rooms, one of them used as storage.

The kitchen was roomy, though not large. A small cupboard sat snugly against one wall and a large kitchen range stood firmly against another. At one end stood a table, its bare wood gleaming in the sun that streamed through the window. There were no curtains, no fussing. Things were plain—but polished clean.

Damaris took in every detail of the room and then crossed to the next, the living room. A big stone fireplace took almost all of one wall. Two chairs faced it and between them was a small table on which lay Gil's Bible. There were no rugs on the floor and a lone calendar graced the wall. It looked bare and simple—but homey.

Damaris walked on to the bedroom at the back. It was another simple room. The bed was neatly made, a colorful Navajo blanket spread across the top. Articles of clothing hung from hooks on the wall. There was no clutter.

"Well, I do see what Miss Dover means," grinned Damaris. "It certainly is untrimmed."

But Damaris liked what she saw.

She laid Tootles on the bed and covered her lightly with a corner of the blanket. Then she returned to the kitchen. She wasn't sure if she should wait for Gil or go ahead with dinner preparations. She dawdled for a moment, running her hand over the polished wood of the table. Then she crossed to the window and looked out into the yard.

Gil was on his way in with William hoisted up on his neck. The boy's hands were buried in the depths of Gil's brown curly hair, and Gil's Stetson was falling down over

William's eyes. Even from the distance, Damaris could see the pleased look on the little boy's face. Abbie was bouncing along ahead of Gil, talking excitedly and waving a hand now and then at the corral and its cattle.

The revelation came to Damaris without warning. She lifted a hand to her breast and a little gasp caught in her throat. At that very moment she realized with startling clarity that she loved Gil Lewis. She closed her eyes tightly and put out a hand to stop the room from swirling around her.

She loved him! Her fear of him had long ago changed to comfort, then to respect, then sharing, and a measure of dependency. But when had her feelings turned to love? She had no business loving him. What would she ever do now?

Her first thought was to flee. But that was impossible.

He'll know, she said to herself. *He'll see it in my face and I'll be so embarrassed.*

Then she firmly reprimanded herself. "Be calm," she said aloud and firmly. "You've hidden your feelings before. Surely you can do it again."

So Damaris steeled herself once more and turned back to the big stove. But much of the excitement had gone out of the day. She prayed that it would end quickly and without incident.

It was a long, agonizing day for Damaris. She was glad for the distraction of the children. Tootles awoke from her nap in a sour mood. Even after Damaris fed her dinner, she still fussed and complained. Gil tried to entertain her but she only clung more tightly to Damaris. And Damaris was more than happy to have the excuse of comforting the child.

William, on the other hand, did not wish to leave Gil's side. *He needs a father,* thought Damaris, but that idea only brought more anguish.

Abbie was everywhere, chatting, giggling, exploring, skipping. She was a bundle of energy and a constant talker.

"What's that horse's name?

"Who hoes the garden?

"Do you shoot things with that gun?

"Why do you live here by yourself? Why don't you have a fam'bly?"

And then she turned to Damaris and asked, "How do you use that thing, Mama?" and pointed to the hammock.

Damaris could tell by the quick lift of Gil's head that he had not heard the child call her Mama before.

Damaris willed her voice to be steady. "It's called a hammock," she answered evenly. "Folks lie in it to rest."

"Can I try it?"

Gil took Abbie to the hammock and, after much laughter and scrambling, finally managed to get the young child properly settled. She smiled smugly as Gil gently rocked her back and forth. And then William had to have his turn, and while he rocked, Tootles went to Gil and held up her arms, determined that she would not be left out of the fun.

Finally it was time to go home. Gil placed fresh hay on the floor of the wagon box and spread the blankets over it.

"Unless I miss my guess," he explained, "we are going to have three sleeping children before we get to town."

Damaris nodded. "Maybe four," she replied with a grin.

Gil was right. They hadn't traveled far before all three children were bundled together on the hay bed, sleeping soundly after their exciting day.

They traveled together in silence. Gil seemed deep in thought and Damaris was afraid to speak lest she betray her feelings.

"Do you think it's time we gave Tootles her real name?" Gil surprised Damaris by asking.

Damaris smiled. "I've been thinking of calling her Florrie," she admitted.

"Florrie. I like that. It suits her."

Silence gently enfolded them. In spite of her troubling thoughts and trembling spirit, Damaris felt at peace. She wished she could cling to this moment. They were almost home before Gil spoke again. He seemed hesitant—but determined.

"I've been doing a lot of thinking lately," he said, "and

praying." He cleared his throat before continuing. "Damaris, I—I'd like to marry you—bring you and the kids to the ranch. You are making a—a wonderful mother—but they need a father, too."

Damaris held her breath. Had she heard him correctly or was she simply hearing the expressions of her own heart?

"I—I know I don't know much about—being a pa—but I think I can learn. I heard Abbie call you Mama today. It sounded real good. Like—like real family. The little ones need that."

Suddenly the beautiful spinning world jerked to a stop. She went over the words again in her mind. Was Gil asking her to marry him for the good of the children? He had their welfare in mind—not the promptings of his own heart.

Damaris had to admit that he was right. She did need help with the children. They did need a father. But could she ever, ever, be content to be a wife of "circumstance"? To love him when he didn't love her?

A sob caught in her throat and her hands went up to cover her face. Gil turned and reached his hand toward her.

"Have I misread things?" he asked, his voice husky with emotion.

Damaris nodded, the tears spilling through her fingers.

"I'm—I'm sorry," he whispered. "I thought—I mean I dared to think that—that you might feel the way I do."

Damaris responded with a fresh burst of tears. If only— if only he truly did feel the way she felt. If only he had asked his question because he loved her—not because he felt obligated to help her with the children.

———

The next days were difficult for Damaris. Even the children noticed her preoccupation, her aloofness, her walk with pain.

"Mama, are you sad?" asked Abbie.

Damaris could only nod her head.

Abbie put her small arms around Damaris and whispered gently, "I will hold you," and Damaris cried again.

It was into the second week when Damaris heard a knock on the door late one evening. The children were in bed and Damaris had been sitting in a chair with a garment held idly on her lap. She had not been sewing, simply looking off into space. But when the knock came, she rose quickly. She was not used to callers—and certainly not at such a late hour.

Dusk was settling, but Damaris could still see plainly as she opened the door a crack. It was Gil who stood there, an apologetic smile on his lips, his worn Stetson in his hands.

Damaris opened the door quickly, her thoughts leaping to Miss Dover.

"There's nothing wrong, is there?" she asked anxiously.

Without answer Gil brushed past her and into the house. He tossed his hat onto a nearby chair and turned to face her.

"Yes," he admitted, his head cocked slightly to one side, his eyes burning into hers. "There is! I can't eat. I can't sleep. I can't even do my work."

Damaris felt relief wash over her. It wasn't Miss Dover. But then a new pain constricted her heart. Gil had not accepted her answer. But he still didn't understand her feelings for him. She turned to him, searching for the words to explain. Before she could begin, he placed his hands on her shoulders.

"Are you sure we couldn't make it work?" he pleaded.

She was about to shake her head sadly, when he went on.

"I love you, Damaris. I—I'm asking you again to be my wife. I—I know that I don't have much to offer you, but I promise—you will have—have everything I do have. My love. My devotion. My respect. I—"

Damaris broke his hold on her shoulders and flung herself into his arms. Her own arms encircled his neck and she leaned against his tall frame and cried against his shoulder. She had heard the words she had longed to hear. He loved her.

He held her closely until her sobs lessened, caressing her shoulder, gently sweeping back the straying wisps of her hair, brushing his lips against the top of her head.

When her tears subsided, he took her shoulders again

and eased her back so he could look into her face. "Does this mean yes?" he asked. His teasing made his blue eyes deepen.

Damaris managed a shaky laugh and a nod of her head. "I thought you didn't love me—that you simply were concerned about—" But his finger on her lips stopped further words as he assured her again of his love.

He held her again, and Damaris had never felt more at home—more secure, in her entire life.

"Soon?" he asked against her hair.

"Soon," replied Damaris. "Just as soon as we can make the arrangements."

He kissed the top of her head again. "I'll get right to work on it," he said. Then he added with merriment, though his words held seriousness too, "I've a mind that Mother is going to like the idea of bein' a grandma."

The thought of the three little ones now being a part of a real family gave Damaris great pleasure. She gazed at Gil with glowing dark eyes and nodded her head.

"She'll make a wonderful grandma," she said. "And I can't wait to write my own mama—and Pa—about you—about us. *Our* family. She'll—they'll be so happy that—that God has been so good."

She leaned against his shoulder again, feeling protected, loved, and at peace.